1629

DATE DUE

Danny Orlis

THE CASE OF
THE TALKING ROCKS

BERNARD PALMER

Tyndale House
Publishers, Inc.
Wheaton, Illinois

Bernard Palmer is also the well-known author of the Breck Western Series and My Son, My Son. *He lives with his wife, Marjorie, in Holdrege, Nebraska.*

The Danny Orlis Adventure Series
The Final Touchdown
The Last Minute Miracle
The Race Against Time
The Showdown
The Case of the Talking Rocks
The Sacred Ruins

Previously published by Moody Press under the title
Danny Orlis and the Rocks that Talk

Library of Congress Catalog Card Number 88-51651
ISBN 0-8423-0559-9
© 1955 by Bernard Palmer
All rights reserved
Printed in the United States of America
95 94 93 92
9 8 7 6 5 4 3

Contents

ONE
A secret mission

Danny Orlis stepped quietly to the door of the log cabin along Pine Creek at Angle Inlet, Minnesota, and went out into the chill, early morning, August air. Little wisps of fog had risen from the water and were floating eerily some three or four feet above the mirrored surface of the bay.

A lone mallard drake wheeled silently past and dropped quietly into the patch of wild rice on the far side of the creek to feed. A hundred yards or so to the left a muskrat poked his furry nose out of the water and began to move noiselessly upstream. The little animal swam lazily, furrowing the water and sending ripples across the surface in an ever-widening V.

A fish splashed in the mouth of the creek as it broke water to gulp down a fly. From the neighbor's clearing behind the post office came the quick, nervous challenge of a terrier who was barking valiantly at some imaginary intruder.

Danny took a deep breath and stood momentarily, staring hungrily about, as though to capture the quiet beauty of the Lake of the Woods and store it in the deep recesses of his heart against the day when he would no longer be where he could feast upon it.

Danny had gotten up almost at dawn and had supposed that the rest of the family were still asleep, but as he looked out toward the dock to where the "Scappoose" was tied, he saw that his younger brother, Ron, was already up and out in the little boat.

Danny walked slowly out to where Ron was sitting. The younger boy was so busy cleaning out the "Scappoose" and stowing his fishing tackle beside him that he did not hear Danny come up until he spoke.

"Hi, Ron!" Danny said.

Ron straightened suddenly and turned, half standing in the boat.

"What's the matter?" Danny laughed. "What do you think you're going to do?"

"Man, you scared me," Ron said, sighing with relief. "I thought maybe Uncle Harold had come back after Roxie and me."

"I don't think you need to worry about that," Danny told him. "Your Uncle Harold isn't going to bother you anymore. It's been proven now that you are legally adopted. You're a part of the family, just as though you had been born into it."

Ron leaned forward to check the fuel gauge on the tank of the new outboard motor. He and Danny had bought it together with some of the money which they had earned in guiding fishermen that summer.

"You know, Danny," he said impulsively, "whenever I think of how close Uncle Harold came to making Roxie and me go and live with him, I feel weak all over. Just think, if he'd gotten away with it, we might

8

never have seen you, or Mother and Dad, or all of this again." He made a wide, expressive sweep with his hand.

"It gave us all a bad time for a while, Ron," Danny said, nodding. "But the Lord was watching over us. We were awfully worried, but we didn't need to be. God was working things out."

"I guess so." Ron picked up his rod and reel and began to tie a leader to the line. "But I sure felt better when it was all over."

"I did too."

"Want to go fishing with me, Danny? I'm going out after some walleyes and jacks right after breakfast." He looked up and grinned. "You know, we'll have to get at this fishing business. In about a month now we'll have to go away to school and won't get to fish, or hunt, or anything."

Danny squatted down on the dock beside the "Scappoose". "I guess that's right," he said. "I know just how you feel, having to think about leaving here for a few months. It used to get me that way, too. The fact is, it still does."

Ron looked to see that he had a pair of pliers, a stout steel stringer, and the gaff hook in the boat. Then he swung himself up on the dock and sat down beside his older brother. The two of them talked for a few minutes about school down in Cedarton and how good it was that Danny was going to the Bible Institute there. They were still talking when Mrs. Orlis came to the cabin door and called them in to breakfast.

When they had eaten and had finished their morning devotions, Ron asked Danny again about going fishing with him, but Mr. Orlis intervened.

"I'd rather you didn't go this morning, Danny," he said, turning to the older boy. "There are some things you and I should attend to."

"I'll help with the work, Dad," Ron put in quickly. "Then Danny and I can both go fishing. Or maybe you can go along. We won't have a chance to do that again until next spring, you know."

Mr. Orlis shook his head. "You and Roxie can go out fishing, son," he said. "I'm going to need Danny this morning."

It did seem strange to Danny that his dad had not wanted him to go fishing with Ron. It was true that there was a great deal of work that needed to be done, but the load of lumber was coming up on the "Empress", and they could not do much about putting the partitions in that new cabin until it arrived.

Then, too, his dad made no effort to move around, even after they had finished eating. He sat down in the big chair beside the radio, listening to the Back to the Bible Broadcast, following the text of the message in his Bible.

The twins listened, too, as they did the dishes. As soon as Mrs. Orlis finished putting up their sandwiches for lunch, they went hurrying out to the dock.

"Sure wish you could go along, Danny," Ron said to him as he went out the door.

"You be careful, fella," Danny cautioned.

"And be back in by noon," Mrs. Orlis said, coming to the door of the kitchen.

As soon as the broadcast was over, Mr. Orlis switched off the radio and turned to Danny.

"There are some things I want to talk over with you,

Danny," he began. "I thought it would be better if the twins were out of the way."

"Is it something about their Uncle Harold?" Danny asked quickly. "I thought all that was settled."

"It is settled," Carl Orlis replied. "At least we don't have to worry about his getting custody of the twins. But there is something else that might be very important." He paused momentarily and turned to look out the window. "Have they gone?" he asked, breaking into what he had been saying.

Danny walked over to the door. "They're just climbing into the 'Scappoose' now," he said. "I don't think they'll be back."

"Fine," his dad replied. He waited until Danny had gone back to the divan and had sat down again. "You know, Danny, I've been trying and trying to figure out why Harold Bauer was so anxious to get the twins. It certainly wasn't because he thought anything of them and was afraid they weren't receiving proper treatment. He didn't even check into the way we have been caring for them until a few weeks ago."

Mrs. Orlis came into the living room and sat down beside Danny.

"Maybe he wants to get his hands on their money," Danny put in.

"That could be," his dad said, "if there were any money. That cement-block factory in Iron Mountain, which the twins' dad operated, went broke after he died. There was a little insurance money, but I don't think there's enough left in the estate to raise the twins and educate them if it were to be used for that purpose."

"Then why would Harold want them?" Danny

asked. Carl Orlis stared for a moment or two at the floor. Finally he looked up.

"The only thing that's left, Danny," he went on slowly, "is about two thousand acres of wasteland in the mountains. When I was made trustee for the twins, I had a man look into the value of the land. He said there was some question in his mind as to whether it was even worth keeping up the taxes, but I felt that we had a Christian obligation to do that much until we sold it, at least."

"If that's the case, though," Mrs. Orlis put in, "why would Harold go to such lengths to try to get the twins?"

"That is the thing we must find out. Harold Bauer is shrewd and ruthless. He had a reason for trying so hard to receive custody of the twins, and if I know him at all, I would say that the reason was money."

"I don't get it," Danny said.

"I was reading in one of the newsmagazines yesterday," Mr. Orlis continued, "that a new highway is being surveyed across the mountains west of Iron Mountain. They are going to start buying right away and build it within a few months—a four-lane, all-surface road."

He paused and picked up the atlas, which was opened to the Colorado map, and traced the location of the new highway with his pencil. "As nearly as I can figure from the account, the road is to go right along here. It's going to run very close to the land which belongs to the twins. If it should happen to run through their land, it will become very valuable."

Danny nodded. "It would have to be something like that to make Harold even want Ron and Roxie. But where do I come into this?"

"We can't find out anything by writing out there," Mr. Orlis answered. "We'll have to make a trip to Iron Mountain and find out about the location of the highway and see just how close it is going to come to the land. I could ask Uncle Claude to do it for me, but he's so busy that I hate to bother him. I thought perhaps you could go back to Iron Mountain and look it over for us."

"You mean you want me to do it?" Danny asked.

"I know you have a lot of things you want to do before you go back to Cedarton to school," his dad said. "But you could fly from Minneapolis and probably find out what the situation is in two or three weeks."

"Boy, that would be great!" Danny said eagerly. "I've been wanting to go back to Iron Mountain to see Larry and Bob and all the gang I used to go to school with, anyway."

"Fine," Carl Orlis said, smiling.

"But, Carl," Danny's mother protested, her face serious "do you think that's wise? You know Harold Bauer and how desperate he can be."

"But Danny wouldn't even have to see Harold," his dad said. "He'll go out to the county seat town of Scranton, west of Iron Mountain, look up the location of the land, and find out about the highway and how far away from the twins' property it will be. He won't even have to go over the place if he doesn't want to."

"I know," Mrs. Orlis answered, "but I just don't trust Harold."

Danny turned to his mother. "You don't need to worry, Mother," he said. "I can take care of myself, all right."

He tried to sound carelessly nonchalant about it,

but when they finally finished talking and he went out on the dock to see if he could pick up the twins with the field glasses, he was strangely ill at ease. He knew Harold Bauer only too well. The fact that he had been blocked in his efforts to gain custody of the twins would not hinder him at all if there were some other way to get what he wanted. The very fact that he had been stopped might make him all the more difficult. In spite of himself, Danny shuddered.

His dad came up behind him just then.

"Danny," he said softly, "I just wanted to tell you that I think it would be best for us not to mention this to the twins. We'll just tell them that you're making the trip to take care of some business for me."

"Sure thing, Dad."

"And, Danny," he added hesitantly, "I didn't want to say anything in front of your mother, because I don't want her to worry; but don't tell anyone why you're out at Scranton, and keep your eyes open for Harold every minute. He's a tough customer."

TWO
Missing reservations

After Carl Orlis and Danny had decided that Danny should go to Iron Mountain and check the tract of mountain land which had been left to the twins, Danny radioed Tex and had his pilot friend phone the airport for plane reservations to the Colorado community.

"Get them as quickly as you can, Tex," he said, "and then plan on coming to pick me up the day before I'm to leave."

Ron had come into the porch, where they kept the radio transmitter, in time to hear Danny mention the reservations.

"Where are you going, Danny?" he asked, disappointment in his voice.

"Down to Iron Mountain to look after some things for Dad."

"Do you have to go?" he asked. "I thought we would be able to get a lot of fishing done in the next couple of weeks."

Tex made the reservations for Danny for the following Tuesday morning and flew up to the Angle to take him down to Minneapolis on Monday afternoon.

Carl Orlis followed him out to the plane. "I want you to be careful now, Danny," he said seriously, lowering his voice so that the rest of the family could not hear. "Remember what I told you about keeping your eyes open, too. Harold might pop up anywhere."

"Don't worry about me, Dad," Danny assured him.

"All set, Danny?" Tex asked, leaning forward to turn on the switch.

"All set." He said good-bye hurriedly, swung up into the little amphibious plane, and pulled the door shut.

They landed at Wold Chamberlain Field, and Danny went into the terminal to verify his reservations before going into town to find a room for the night.

"Just a moment, Mr. Orlis," the attractive young lady behind the desk said, smiling. "I'll check to see that your reservations are here and in order."

She picked up the telephone and repeated the information to someone in another part of the building.

"But it can't be!" she was saying. "He's right here now. . . . Just a moment—I'll talk to him." She put her hand over the phone and turned to Danny. "The office says that you picked up your reservation and ticket early this morning."

"But I didn't!" Danny protested. "I just got in. I couldn't have picked them up."

The girl looked quite perplexed. "Would you mind coming in and talking with our reservations clerk, Mr. Orlis?" she asked. "There must be some mistake."

He followed her to one of the inner offices, where a tall, black-haired man was sitting.

"The reservation and ticket for Danny Orlis were picked up this morning," he said, eyeing Danny critically, "just after I came on duty. I took care of it myself."

"But I'm Danny Orlis," Danny repeated.

"The Orlis reservation was phoned in from Baudette," he said, bristling. "This Orlis chap was here half a dozen times this past week to see if it had come in. It seems that the same party who made the reservation was to wire him money for the ticket. He came in this morning with the money, bought his ticket, and picked up the reservation."

"But I'm Orlis."

The clerk got to his feet. "I'm sorry," he said coldly. Danny stood there for a moment, bewildered. Who could possibly want his plane reservation? And why?

"Is—is there any chance of getting a reservation for Iron Mountain tonight or tomorrow?" he asked numbly.

The clerk shook his head. "Our flights are booked solid for the next four days."

"But I must get to Iron Mountain right away."

"I'm sorry." The clerk simpered once more, a thin smile toying with the corner of his mustache.

Danny allowed the girl who had accompanied him to lead him back out into the terminal.

"The flights are booked solid all right," she said to him, "but I'll tell you what you might do. Hang around until plane time. There might be some cancellations. If there are any, I'll see if I can save one for you."

"Thanks," he told her.

Danny went over to one corner of the long, busy terminal and sat down on a bench. There were four flights to Iron Mountain that night. That meant that he would have to sit there and wait, hoping against hope that he might be able to get a cancellation.

Who besides Harold Bauer would have made an effort to take his reservation for Iron Mountain? Danny's mind was reeling. But what would Harold be doing now in the Twin Cities? True, he had been in the area a scant two weeks before, but everyone had supposed that he had headed directly back to Colorado after the Orlises had gotten the twins from him and he saw that there was no chance of getting them back. Besides, how could Harold have found out that Danny was going to make the trip to Iron Mountain? There were a hundred unanswered questions in his mind.

Danny walked to the door to watch a Boeing stratocruiser, just in from Seattle, roll up and stop.

It was tiresome waiting to see about possible cancellations. The flights were several hours apart, and Danny was afraid to let himself drop off to sleep for fear he would miss his chance to catch a plane. That was just what happened shortly after midnight. The first two flights were full, but he had fallen asleep momentarily when a cancellation was announced for the one-o'clock plane. It was snatched up before he even knew about it.

The next plane did not leave until six-thirty in the morning. It was the one which he thought he had reservations for, but this time he was determined not to miss any cancellations there might be. He went into the coffeeshop and ate heavily. Having bought a magazine, he forced himself to read the hunting and fishing articles until almost five o'clock.

Danny put aside his magazine and sleepily looked at his watch. Instantly he was wide awake. If Harold Bauer was the one who had gotten his reservation, he would be coming out to the airport soon! Danny would have to go off in a corner somewhere so that he would not be seen. Danny grinned self-consciously. A lot of good that would do if there happened to be a cancellation. They would be on the same plane. Besides, he told himself, there was no use in trying to hide. If Harold had his reservations, he knew that Danny was going to Iron Mountain and probably why. Nevertheless, his heart was beating a violent tattoo against his shirt as he went up to the desk and asked about cancellations.

"I think I have some good news for you," the girl at the desk said, running her finger down the passenger list. "A man by the name of Orlis phoned that he was having to postpone his trip."

"Orlis?" Danny echoed.

"That's right. Somebody by the name of Danny Orlis." Danny scarcely remembered what he said, or buying his own ticket, or even paying for it. The girl had started suddenly when he told her his name and asked him to repeat it.

"I've never had that happen before," she said, looking at the passenger list once more.

Danny mumbled something under his breath and picked up his ticket and his change.

Perhaps it was not Harold, after all, he reasoned. Perhaps there had been a whole series of mix-ups that ended with his getting his seat. Or—he shivered at the thought—perhaps Harold had only wanted to find out whether or not he was going to Iron Mountain and was taking this means of blocking him. Almost involuntarily Danny looked about him, half expecting to see Harold Bauer come striding up to where he was standing. As soon as the Denver and Iron Mountain flight was announced, he climbed on board.

Danny had wired Larry, his cousin, before getting on the DC-7 that flew to Denver, where he had to change to a smaller plane for the short hop to Iron Mountain.

Uncle Claude and all the family were at the airport in Iron Mountain when he landed. Aunt Lydia kissed him. Bob, Larry, and Uncle Claude shook his hand heartily. For the moment Danny forgot about Harold and the strange incident that had taken place at the airport in Minneapolis.

"It's good to see you, Danny," Larry said over and over, grinning widely as he reached down for the suitcase. "It's so good to see you."

"I'll say it is," Uncle Claude agreed.

"It's good to be here, too," Danny said. He had not thought that he was homesick for the small Colorado town, but now that he was here, he felt his heart warm. He looked quickly about. "The old place is just about the same, isn't it?"

"Just about the same," Uncle Claude replied. "We're the ones who are different since you were here."

Danny looked at him quizzically, not understanding what he meant for a moment.

"We didn't know what it was to really live," Uncle Claude went on, "until we accepted Christ as our Savior and began to live for him."

"That's great," Danny answered.

Larry looked the same as he always had. He was a little taller and a little heavier perhaps, but he had that same jaunty set to his shoulders and the same quick smile and dancing blue eyes.

They went home presently, and Aunt Lydia finished dinner while Danny and the others sat in the living room talking rapidly. It was not until bedtime, when Danny and Larry were alone together in the basement room that Danny had when he stayed there and went to school, that Danny told his cousin the purpose of his trip to Colorado.

"But why would anyone want to fight for land out west of Scranton, Danny?" Larry asked. "Dad and Bob and I went fishing out that way a couple of times last year. You ought to see that country. It's the wildest place you ever saw. And rough to get to! Man, it almost takes a cross between a mountain goat and an eagle to get over that trail!"

"It's just a guess," Danny told him. "Dad was basing it on what he knew about Harold and on a thing or two he let drop. It might be that there isn't anything to it. That's one of the things we'll have to find out."

"We'll get in some good trout fishing, anyway," Larry laughed. "I don't think we'll find anything else."

Danny Orlis looked furtively about and leaned forward. "Just the same," he went on, "Harold has some reason for not wanting me to come out here." Hurriedly he told Larry what had happened in the air terminal in Minneapolis.

"Man!" Larry exclaimed, his eyes growing wide. "Maybe there is something to this, after all."

The two boys planned on going to Scranton early the next morning, but on the way downtown they burned out a connecting rod in Larry's old car. The mechanic was so busy that he was not able to get to it for two or three days.

"We just have to have a car up there," Larry said, when Danny suggested going over to Scranton by bus. "I don't know exactly where that land is, but I know that we can save ourselves a lot of hard walking and climbing by taking the car and driving as far as we can. We're going to have enough of that to do."

"It would probably look suspicious, anyway," Danny said, "if we strike off the minute I get to town."

While they were waiting for the car to be fixed, the two boys made the rounds of all Danny's old friends.

"How's Peggy Denton?" he asked as they left one of the guys' homes late that afternoon.

"She's had two years of Bible school now," Larry replied. "And I think she's going to a Christian college somewhere this fall. She's going to be a missionary."

"And what about Eric Tanner?" Danny asked, remembering the young football player who had accepted a bribe to throw the state championship football game the year he played with Iron Mountain.

Larry shook his head. "He's bitterly against anyone who has anything to do with the Lord," his cousin replied. "He spent nine mouths in the reformatory the first time, and I think he's been in jail two or three times since."

They were still talking about Eric, when a car went speeding past them up the highway.

"There goes Eric now!" Larry exclaimed. "He's driving that car!"

But Danny was not listening. His face had turned

white, and beads of sweat were standing out on his forehead.

"What's the matter?" Larry demanded.

"Did you see who was with him?" Danny asked.

His cousin shook his head. "Why?"

"I thought it was Harold Bauer!"

THREE
Mysterious pursuers

Danny Orlis and his cousin Larry stood for a moment or two, staring blankly after the car that had just passed them.

"Do you really think that was Harold and Eric?" Larry asked excitedly. "Are you sure?"

"It certainly looked like them," Danny replied thoughtfully. "I think I'd recognize that face of Harold's anywhere. But I got just a glimpse of him. I couldn't be positive."

Larry pushed his cap to the back of his head and ran his fingers through his hair. "I don't get it," he said. "You tell me that you're sure he was in Minneapolis yesterday. Then how could he be here today?"

"He could have come the same way I did," Danny answered, "taking a later plane, maybe. But that doesn't make sense, either. If he was planning to come here to Iron Mountain, why didn't he keep my reservation when he had it?"

By this time the Tanner car had stopped at a stoplight, three or four blocks up the street. The driver signaled for a left turn, and the car moved slowly out of sight.

"It just doesn't fit," Danny said at last. "Nothing fits."

They crossed the street in silence and started up an alley to take a short cut to the home of a new friend whom Larry wanted Danny to meet.

"Come to think of it," Danny said suddenly, "I could be mistaken about Harold. I got just a glimpse of him, and he was wearing a hat." He laughed self-consciously. "I guess I'm so jumpy that I'll probably be seeing Harold in every automobile and behind every billboard until after we get up to Scranton and finish our job."

As the two boys walked up to the Carson house, a tall, sandy-haired guy about Larry's age came out on the porch and grinned pleasantly.

"Hi, Larry!" he called out when he saw them. "I've been trying to get you on the phone all afternoon."

Larry introduced Danny to Jerry—"Kit"—Carson, and the three of them sat down on the porch steps.

"Thought maybe you'd like to go with me up to the Box Y ranch for two or three days, Larry," Kit said to Danny's cousin. "We could get in a little trout fishing."

"Danny and I have to go over to Scranton on business."

"Scranton?" Kit echoed. "That's only three or four miles from the ranch. Why don't we go together?"

Larry looked over at Danny quizzically. There was something about Kit that Danny liked almost instinctively. He had a quick, ready smile and a clean, honest look.

"My car is broken down," Larry answered, still eyeing his cousin for a sign. "I don't know whether that would suit Danny or not, but it would mean that we'd be able to get to Scranton two or three days sooner than we will if we wait for my car to be repaired."

Kit grinned, looking toward the red-and-yellow jalopy that was parked in the driveway. "We could try my car," he said, "but I've got to warn you—the last three times I went anywhere we all wound up pushing."

Danny was silent for a moment. What had his dad said about letting anyone other than Larry know why he had come to Colorado? He had not even told Bob, or Uncle Claude, or Aunt Lydia. Yet Kit was a nice guy, and he would not have to tell him very much about their trip—just enough to satisfy his curiosity. Besides, if Harold was in the area, he would be going to Scranton soon; and Kit could have Danny and Larry there at least two days earlier.

"I'm willing to take a chance on the pushing," Danny laughed, "if you'll guarantee to deliver us there."

"Sure thing, even if you have to walk every foot of the way."

When Danny, Larry, and Kit had finished making their plans for the trip, the two cousins left and started toward home.

"I'm surely glad that we're taking Kit along, Danny," Larry said.

"I hope we don't have to tell him too much about our trip and why we're going."

"You won't need to worry about Kit. He's all right."

"Just the same, I don't think we ought to tell anyone about it. That's the only way we can be sure there won't be any leaks," Danny told him.

"I've been with Kit quite a lot the past three or four months," Danny's cousin went on. "I've been trying to talk with him about spiritual things and accepting Christ as his Savior. I thought maybe we'd have a good chance to talk with him on a trip like this."

"I might have known there was something like that," Danny said, "to make you want so badly to have him along."

Early the next morning Danny and Larry got up and gathered their things together. Aunt Lydia wanted to fix breakfast for them, but the boys would not hear of it. Danny fried a couple of eggs and some bacon while Larry set the table.

They had just started to eat when Kit rattled up in his old car and leaned on the horn. Larry jumped to his feet.

"Wait a minute, fella," Danny protested. "I haven't finished eating."

"I'll get out there and hold Kit down," Larry told him, wriggling into his jacket. "If I don't, he'll have everyone in the neighborhood awake."

The boys threw Larry's tent and a couple of sleeping bags into the backseat of Kit's car, and in a moment or two they were driving up the narrow, twisting road which led over the mountains to Scranton. Kit had not been exaggerating when he had voiced his doubts that his car would be able to make it up the gravel mountain road. It wheezed and rattled and groaned from low to second and back to low again.

"There's one thing about going out in the car with me," Kit laughed as he shifted again. "You never know just how far you're going or what will happen next."

"You can say that again," Larry told him, laughing.

"We can always walk," Danny put in.

"Now if something actually happened to Nellie, you guys wouldn't go off and leave me all by myself, would you?" the driver asked with mock sincerity. "After all, she's the only car I've got."

"Tell you what we'll do, Kit," Danny's cousin said, grinning widely, "if you have any real trouble with her, we'll keep you in mind on the way back from Scranton. And if you're still out here, we'll stop and hold your hand for a while."

"Just like a pal, don't you think, Danny?" The radiator started to boil, and Kit filled it from a five-gallon can of water which he carried in the trunk. When he climbed back in the car, he turned to Danny again.

"Yes, sir," he said, "Larry is OK. Only thing is, he's preaching to a guy all the time. Does he do that to you, too?"

"To tell you the truth, Kit," Larry said seriously, "Danny is the one who preached to me first."

Kit turned quickly to face Danny. "No," he exclaimed, "that can't be!"

"That's right," Larry went on. "You should have seen how I was living when Danny came along."

The smile left Kit's face. "I'd certainly never believe that if you hadn't told me yourself, Larry," he said at last. "If I've ever met a guy who I thought had never done anything out of the way, it's you. Why, you don't even go to parties and dances at school."

"I'm certainly not proud of my old life," Danny's cousin told him. "But it's the truth. That's the sort of life I had been living. When Danny came, I saw that there was another way to live." He took a deep breath. "Up until that time I'd always felt that anyone who didn't curse and smoke and lie and steal was a sissy. I got all fouled up because I wouldn't listen to what Danny tried to tell me about the Lord Jesus. I even had to serve another stretch at the reformatory. But then I accepted Christ as my personal Savior, and everything has been different since."

Kit moistened his lips with the tip of his tongue and once or twice started to speak but stopped thoughtfully.

"That's why the Lord means so much to me," Larry explained. "I know what sort of life I'd be living and where I'd be heading if it hadn't been for Christ."

There was another awkward silence. Kit devoted his attention to the car, and for another quarter of a mile or so no one spoke.

"I didn't do quite the same things that Larry had done before he became a Christian," Danny said at last, "but I can tell you this much, Kit—the Lord means a great deal to me, too. He has watched over me and cared for me day by day. He has made a big difference in my life."

For almost an hour the guys jounced over the narrow, rock-strewn mountain road without saying very much. They had been talking a great deal before, but now they sat there thoughtfully, staring out over the majestic hills or looking behind them down into the valley.

Finally they pulled into Scranton—a small, dirty little coal-mining town with narrow streets and gloomy, unpainted houses. The village clung precariously to the side of the hill, as though it were in imminent danger of slipping off into the river, a thousand feet below.

"There!" Kit sighed as he stopped at the town's only stop sign. "We made it! We got here in this old heap without having something fall off."

"We really accomplished something," Larry laughed.

"I was just thinking," Danny said. "Why don't you guys take me over to the courthouse? I'll see the county clerk while you find out if your pal's out at the ranch, Kit."

The driver of the car started to voice his protest, but Larry spoke quickly. "That's a good idea, Danny," he said. "I'm glad you thought of it." He knew the reason why Danny wanted to have Kit out of the way.

Kit and Larry let Danny out of the car in front of the weatherbeaten courthouse and went clattering off up the street. Danny went into the building and found the county clerk's office.

"What property did you say you're interested in?" the girl at the desk asked him.

"It belongs to the Bauer estate," he repeated. "It's a tract of mountain land, about two thousand acres, as I remember it."

"Would that be the Harold Bauer—" She checked herself hurriedly, her face flushing. "I mean," she corrected, "the John Bauer tract?"

"That's right," Danny said.

She stood for a moment or two, staring at him uncertainly, then went over toward the window. Her hands were trembling as she fingered a pencil on the desk.

"I'm awfully sorry," she said evasively, "but I'm afraid I won't be able to help you, after all. You'll have to see Mr. Clarkson. He's familiar with the books and can probably give you the information you wish."

"But they told me that if I came here, I could find out about it," Danny said. "The deed is supposed to be recorded."

"You will have to talk to Mr. Clarkson." With that she turned abruptly into the vault behind her before Danny could ask her another question.

He stood there uncertainly for a moment or two, wanting to ask her when the county clerk would be back, but she busied herself in the vault and would not come out until the door opened and a short, graying man came bustling into the office.

"Mr. Clarkson," she said, coming out of the vault and addressing the newcomer, "this young man would like some information about the Bauer land."

The county clerk hung up his hat and took off his glasses, staring suspiciously at Danny.

"Why do you want to find out about the Bauer land?" the county clerk demanded.

Danny was silent.

"What do you want to know about that property?" the man repeated, his gaze boring into the young man.

"I wanted to find out whether or not the new highway was going to cut across it," Danny stammered. "I figured on inquiring a little around town about it after I found out just where it's located."

A smile came across the clerk's face. "You won't be able to find out anything about it here in Scranton," he said, warming suddenly.

Danny's face showed his disappointment.

"Nobody around here knows a thing about it," the man went on. "Those fellows came in here and went right up into the hills without saying a word." He leaned across the desk. "They're up in that area right now. If you go up there, you can probably see them and find out everything you want to know."

"Do you suppose they would tell me?" Danny asked.

"They wouldn't have to," he replied. "If the road's running through the Bauer property, they'll have their stakes up. You can't miss."

A wide smile broke across Danny's face. "Thanks," he said. "Thanks a lot."

Mr. Clarkson disappeared into the vault and came out with a heavy, clothbound book. Danny moved over to the desk to take a look at the record book, but Mr. Clarkson turned it deliberately so that he could not see and began to thumb through the pages.

"Yes," he said after a time, "that land is in sections 28, 29, and 30 in Bear Mountain Township. It hasn't changed hands for over thirty years. That's why I didn't remember it."

Danny wrote down the description of the land.

"And now," he asked respectfully, "could you tell me how to get there?"

"I don't rightly know," Mr. Clarkson hedged, "without doing some figuring." He closed the heavy book and came around to the other side of the desk, where Danny was standing. "Here," he said, "I'll give you directions. If you follow them, you shouldn't have any trouble getting out there."

Danny listened carefully, thanked him, and left.

As he came out of the courthouse, he saw a car turn the corner hurriedly and speed away. His heart stopped, fluttering in a sudden spasm of fear, and then leaped to his throat, and began to hammer wildly.

That car! It looked exactly like the one Eric Tanner had been driving!

FOUR
Telephone threat

Danny Orlis was still standing there staring after the car when Larry and Kit drove up.

"What's the matter with you?" Kit demanded as Danny stepped into the car. "You look like you've just seen a ghost."

"Maybe I have," Danny said wryly, managing a crooked little grin. "I just thought I saw Eric Tanner's car go down the street."

Kit looked at him quizzically. "What's so strange about that? That's what the street's for, isn't it?"

"Did you get your business attended to, Danny?" Larry asked quickly.

Danny nodded. "I found out a little of what I wanted to know," he said. "But I still don't know whether it's actually going to help any."

Kit pulled over to the side of the street and stopped abruptly.

"Listen, guys," he said, turning to face them, "I've had about all of this that I can take. Come on, loosen up a little. What gives?"

Larry colored slightly, and he turned from Kit to stare at his cousin. "What about it, Danny?" he asked softly, his lips scarcely forming the words.

Danny was silent for the space of a minute. "I think we owe you some sort of explanation, Kit," he said hesitantly.

"I guess you do," Kit exclaimed determinedly. "Here I've been waiting patiently for you to unburden your-selves ever since we left home this morning. But now I've had all I can take. If I don't find out what this is all about, we don't move a wheel on old Nellie."

Hurriedly Danny told Kit Carson about Harold—how the twins' uncle had tried his best to get custody of them, even going so far as to kidnap them and take them up to Canada. He told how, after the Orlises had them back, his dad had wanted him to come to Iron Mountain to investigate the tract of land that had been left for Ron and Roxie.

"That's the only thing we can think of that might be valuable enough to cause Harold to fight for the twins," Danny concluded.

Kit whistled in amazement. "So that's it!" he exclaimed. "No wonder you're so careful about letting anyone find out why you're here."

"And," Larry put in excitedly, "Danny and I thought we saw Eric and Harold together yesterday afternoon in Eric's car. That's why Danny was so excited when he thought he saw that same car here in Scranton."

Kit whistled again.

"We know you won't tell anybody about this," Danny said to him. "It's awfully important that we keep it as quiet as possible. If Harold knows we're out here, we don't want him to even suspect the real reason for our coming."

"So," Larry cut in with the frankness of friendship, "just keep that big mouth of yours shut about it, even over at the dude ranch where you're going to visit."

"Who's going to visit at a dude ranch?" Kit demanded. "If you think you can get rid of me after telling me all of this stuff, you've got another guess coming. After all, I'm responsible for hauling you guys up here."

"Well," Danny told him, "we can surely use you."

"I should think so. You might have to use old Nellie as a getaway car if the going is tough," Kit laughed.

It was too late that evening for the boys to start back into the mountains to inspect the twins' land, so they went out to the dude ranch and made arrangements to use three saddle horses and a couple of pack animals.

"Now," Danny observed as they climbed back into the car, "we can get a good start in the morning."

The boys left their gear at the ranch and went back to Scranton, where they spent the night at a motel. Before going to bed, Larry picked up the Gideon Bible from the dresser and opened it to the place in Ephesians where he had been reading for his personal devotions.

"Why don't we have our Bible reading together, Danny?" he asked, going over to the chair by the desk and sitting down.

Kit Carson looked over at him almost suspiciously. "If you're doing this for my benefit, you can save your breath," he retorted shortly.

"We make it a habit to read the Bible every night before we go to bed," Danny told him. "You just happen to be here, that's all."

"Oh," Kit replied, "I thought maybe you guys were getting ready to put the squeeze on me."

While Larry read from the New Testament, Kit lay on the bed and suddenly became engrossed in an outdoor magazine. Nevertheless, Danny noticed that every once in a while Kit stopped reading and was listening. When the two boys had finished reading and got down on their knees to pray, Kit coughed nervously, jumped noisily to his feet, and strode outside.

"Where do you suppose he went?" Danny asked when they had finished praying and were undressing.

"He acts that way almost every time I mention the Lord to him," Larry said. "We'll have to pray for him, Danny. He's a good kid, but he needs the Lord Jesus as his personal Savior."

The next morning the three boys were up at dawn. They drove out to the dude ranch, where they left their car, took the saddle horses and pack mules which the ranch foreman had lent them, and started off into the hills toward the place where the county clerk had said the Bauer land lay.

The trail which they started up was wide and well traveled for the first several miles, and it looked as though they would have an easy time going up to inspect the timberland. However, the trail began to narrow until it became only a cow path, winding through the trees along the sheer granite cliffs and up the mountainside at such a dizzying climb that Danny, who was not used to high places, felt his head swimming.

"Are you sure we're on the right path?" Larry asked for the third or fourth time, as the morning gave way to noon.

"I'm sure we're following the directions that the county clerk gave me," Danny said.

"You mean you think we're following the directions he gave you," Kit chided.

"This time I know," Danny answered, laughing. "I've had to follow a lot of trails back home and a good many directions in the woods. I'm positive that we haven't made a mistake."

They stopped for lunch on the trail, taking time only to cook some coffee and warm a can of beans.

"Do you think we'll find Harold when we get there?" Larry asked as they climbed on their horses and started up once more.

"I don't think this Harold guy is even going to be able to find the place," Kit laughed. "The fact is, I think we're lost—good and lost."

"We're still on the trail Mr. Clarkson told me about," Danny said.

But for the first time Danny began to waver a little. It was true that not very many people found their way back into the mountains to the Bauer land, but Clarkson had said that the trail was quite well traveled. He had said that there would be landmarks along the way—a glimpse of Dugan's Peak, off to the left, just after they skirted the cliff, and the granite rock slide on the other side of the valley, halfway up the mountain. Danny stopped uncertainly and looked around.

"What's the matter?" Kit asked, smiling broadly. "Are you getting ready to admit that we are lost?"

"I don't know," Danny answered, more bewildered than ever. "I'm sure I followed those directions he gave me. I took special care to get everything straight. I even asked him to repeat them, because I know what it's like to be lost out in country like this. But I have to admit that something's wrong."

Larry reined in sharply. "I've been wondering about that for a couple of hours, Danny," he said. "I haven't seen any of those things that this country clerk told you we'd be seeing."

"The trouble is," Kit repeated, "that we don't have a very good guide. We should have brought somebody from the ranch. Then we'd have found the place."

Danny looked at him quickly. The twinkle in Kit's eye revealed the fact that he was joking.

"I don't believe there's any use in our going any farther," Danny said. "We must be on the wrong trail."

"Do you suppose we can even find our way back?" Kit taunted, turning his horse around. "It would be terrible if we couldn't find town."

"That's what these horses are for," Danny answered. "They tell me that dude-ranch horses always go home when it gets dark, so we don't have anything to worry about."

"Well," Kit said, "it's a mighty good thing that the horses know something about directions. It's pretty plain that someone else in our party doesn't."

Danny took the kidding good-naturedly.

It was not difficult for them to find their way back down to the dude ranch, but they had traveled so far that it was after dark when they finally reached the ranch and turned their horses into the barn.

"So," Kit exclaimed to his friend who worked there, "we have to go into town and check again to be sure just where this place is that we're looking for. We'll be back for the horses again tomorrow."

"Be careful about what you say about our business here, Kit," Danny cautioned when they were alone in the car again. "It's awfully easy to make people suspicious."

"I'm sorry," Kit replied. "A guy just doesn't realize how hard it is to keep a secret until he begins to try."

The boys rode in silence to the cafe, where they parked and went inside.

"Well," Larry said as he looked at the menu, "there's one thing that we won't have to do until tomorrow— that's cook anything to eat.

"Suits me, too," Kit retorted. "I'm not so much on the cooking end of this business. Just the eating."

The boys had given their order, and the waitress had just come to their table with their salads and milk when the telephone rang and the cafe proprietor came up to them.

"Pardon me," he said as he approached, "but is there a Danny Orlis at this table?"

Danny jumped at the mention of his name.

"I'm Orlis," he said.

"You're wanted on the telephone," the proprietor told him.

"The telephone?" Danny echoed. He looked blankly at his companions. "I don't know how anyone would know that we were here, do you?"

Larry and Kit were as white and tense as Danny was when he went to the telephone at the back of the restaurant.

"Orlis?" a hoarse voice demanded.

"Yes, sir," Danny stammered. "Who is this? What do you want?"

"Don't you worry about who I am," the voice rumbled. "But I'm going to tell you this much. You'd better be on your way out of town the first thing in the morning!"

"Who is this?" Danny asked.

"If you know what's good for you, you'll beat it!" the voice continued. "I tried to keep you from coming down here from Minneapolis, but you wouldn't take my warning. Now I'm going to give you another. If you don't get out of here by an hour after daylight to-morrow, I won't be responsible for what happens!"

With that the receiver on the other end of the line dropped back on the hook. The line was dead.

FIVE
A ghost town

The cafe proprietor, who had been watching Danny at the telephone, came over to him when he had finished.

"What's the matter, son?" he asked. "Is there something wrong? Did you get bad news from home?"

Danny shook his head.

"No," he said, "the message wasn't from home." He started to walk back toward the booth where his friends were sitting. "Thanks for calling me to the phone."

"Who was it?" Larry demanded as he sat down.

"I don't know for sure," Danny said slowly.

"What did they say? What did they want?" Kit questioned.

"It might have been Harold," Danny went on, as though he had not even heard Kit. "But somehow it didn't sound like him."

When he told them what the man on the phone had said, they finished eating hurriedly and went outside.

"Do you suppose it could be Harold?" Larry asked.

"What do you think we ought to do?" Kit asked, all

41

the humor gone from his voice. "We don't dare go back to that motel. If whoever called knew that we were in the cafe just now, he would surely know about the motel."

Danny looked about him quickly. "The fact is," he said lowering his voice, "that proves that we've been followed here. We didn't even know where we were going to eat until we saw the sign and pulled in."

"That means that Harold, or somebody who wants to keep us away from the Bauer land, already knows that we're around."

"And they'll follow us tonight, too," Kit put in, "so they can be sure that we'll leave town the first thing in the morning."

"Maybe we ought to leave now," Larry suggested timidly. "That would throw them off the track."

"We don't dare," Danny said. "I've got a hunch that time means a lot in this deal. We might lose out altogether if we wait."

"Just the same, our skins would be all in one piece," Larry replied.

It was Danny who thought of taking the pack horses and going out into the hills, not far from the ranch house, to sleep in their tent.

"We can start out of town just as though we're going back to Iron Mountain," he said. "Whoever called me, if they're watching us—"

"They're watching, all right," Kit said. "You can be positive of that."

"If they're watching us," Danny repeated, "they'll think that we're scared to death and that we're going back to Iron Mountain. Then we can take that little short cut you were telling us about, Kit, and go back to the ranch house to get our supplies."

"But we haven't found out the exact location of that tract of land yet," Larry said. "We'll have to go back to Scranton for that in the morning."

"I'd just as soon take my chances of facing Harold, or whoever it was who called me, in the daylight tomorrow rather than tonight," Danny answered.

"You can say that again," Kit replied fervently.

If the boys were followed out of Scranton, they succeeded in deceiving their pursuer, for they reached the ranch house without difficulty and slept in the tent, half a mile or so away. The next morning they decided to ride into town on horseback rather than risk being seen in Kit's vivid jalopy, which could be spotted almost as far as the eye could see.

"We'd better stay off the main street," Danny said as they neared the little mountain community. "We can tie our horses over at the general store, where all the dudes from the ranch stop, and walk over to the courthouse from there. That won't excite any suspicion."

The sleepy little town was quiet, except for two or three cars on the main street and a half dozen vacationers from the ranch, who were riding stiffly into town on unfamiliar mounts.

"You guys aren't doing it right," Kit said, urging his horse three or four steps ahead of the others. "You've got to ride like this." He stiffened in the saddle, stuck out his elbows at right angles, and began to jounce painfully with every move of his trotting horse.

"You sure look the part of a dude, all right," Danny and Larry said, laughing.

This time the three of them went into the county

clerk's office to find out about the Bauer land. Mr. Clarkson was apologetic.

"I'm certainly sorry that you weren't able to find it," he said, coming over to where they were standing. He leaned across the counter. "I tried to give you directions that were clear enough so that you could follow them without any trouble."

"Maybe Danny, here, forgot something," Larry laughed. "You know, he's from Minnesota, where they call an ant hill a mountain."

This time Mr. Clarkson checked the directions carefully and repeated them several times for the three boys.

"Now, it isn't difficult at all," he said. "Just go out of town toward the dude ranch and take the first turn to the right. Be sure to take that first turn, and you won't have any difficulty from there on, as far as getting lost is concerned. But you're going to find that you're in for a hard, rugged climb. That isn't the easiest tract of land to reach. I don't know why John Bauer ever persisted in hanging on to it. It can't be used for anything."

Once they were outside the building, Danny turned to his companions. "Now," he said, "if we can just get to our horses and out of town without being seen, we'll be all set."

They almost missed the first turn, despite the fact that all three of them were looking for it. It was a narrow road that looked more like some farmer's land than a trail that went back into the mountains.

Danny had ridden past it, when Kit called out, "Danny, where are you going? Here it is."

They turned and rode up the long, winding trail.

This time there was no mistaking the fact that they were on a regular mountain trail. For the first several miles it was wide enough so that a car could have been driven on it. Then it went off into the trees, narrowing presently; but it was still wide enough for them to be sure that it was a regular path.

All three of them watched for the landmarks, noting each one. It was a steep, hard climb. Before they had been traveling two hours, their horses were wet with sweat.

"Believe me," Danny said as they stopped to rest their mounts, "Mr. Clarkson was certainly right when he said that this was a hard place to get to. That's one thing about our country back home. We don't have to climb like this."

"You just have to swim," Larry retorted.

Kit had stood up and was looking back over the trail, which wound below them like a long, sinuous snake.

"You know," he said, "there's one good thing about all of this. If Harold or anyone else tries to sneak up on us, we can see them coming from a long way off."

"And," Danny added, "if we can see them, they can see us."

Kit's face blanched. "I didn't think of that," he said. There was a long silence.

After a time Larry spoke. "The very fact that Harold has been doing everything he could to keep us from coming to look at this tract of land seems to prove that there's something mighty important and valuable up here."

They stopped for an hour or so at noon, unsaddling their horses and hobbling them to let them rest and eat a little. Danny built a small fire and cooked lunch, and Kit and Larry washed the dishes.

"We must be on the right trail," Larry said about four o'clock. "We've checked off every landmark that Mr. Clarkson gave us, in just the order he gave them."

"That's because there were a couple of real mountaineers in with Danny when he got the information," Kit laughed. "He couldn't get mixed up when you and I were with him, Larry."

They had traveled for another hour or so when Danny caught a glimpse of a shabby, weatherbeaten building through the trees.

"Look up there," he said, pointing.

Half a mile or so ahead were a handful of ramshackled, unpainted buildings, scattered through the trees. Even from where the boys were, they could see that the place was unoccupied.

"Mr. Clarkson didn't say anything about a town up here."

"It—it must be a ghost town," Larry stammered.

"I've been fishing and hunting all over this part of the country," Kit went on, "but I've never heard anyone mention a ghost town up here."

"Maybe it's a mirage," Danny said as they neared the abandoned group of buildings.

"I can't figure it out," Kit repeated. "I just can't figure it out."

"What do you say we stop here for the night and poke around a little?" Danny asked. "We can't possibly get up to the Bauer land today."

"You aren't serious about that, are you?" Larry asked, looking about apprehensively. "You wouldn't actually want to camp in a bunch of old buildings like that, would you?"

"You aren't scared, are you, Larry?" Kit taunted.

"No," his friend told him. "I'm not scared. I'm just careful. I make it a practice to take extra good care of me."

They rode down the narrow street, looking at the buildings on either side. There was an old saloon with one swinging door still in place and a row of glasses on a shelf behind the bar. Next to the building was a hotel, and across the street was the general store, with a faded sign on the front of it that was no longer legible.

"Man!" Larry exclaimed, shivering. "It gives me the creeps just to ride through the place."

They stopped their horses at the general store, hitching them to the post, and went inside.

"I'll bet we're the first customers here in fifty years," Kit laughed. "Wish I could buy a postcard and send it to the folks."

"If you can find a postcard," Danny said, "I don't suppose anyone would object if you helped yourself to it."

There was not much in the store to show what it had been in the years gone by. The counters were there, and there was an old pot-bellied stove in the center of the floor, with the spittoon beside it. In the back was the barrel, which had undoubtedly been used for pickles or crackers in the days when the town was thriving. But the foodstuffs had long since been removed from the shelves to make room for the dust that was piled there.

"I can't understand what you guys see in a place like this," Larry said, turning to glance at the door. "Come on. Let's get out of here."

They went over to the hotel next and then to the saloon.

"You know," Danny said thoughtfully, "these old mountain towns must really have been something. There was at least one saloon in every one of them, and usually three or four. But there weren't any churches. They must have been terribly wild places."

"I'd never thought of that," Larry said, walking over to where Danny was standing. "But that's just the way a lot of people are, too. They make room for all the evil there is in the world. They smoke, and dance, and drink, and gamble, and carouse, but they make sure that the Lord never has a chance to come into their lives. It's no wonder that so many people are like they are."

Kit bristled slightly. "Now listen, guys," he retorted almost sharply, "I'll admit that I'm not as religious as you guys are—the fact is, I'm not religious at all—but I don't do those things you're talking about."

"I'm sorry, Kit," Larry told his friend. "I didn't mean to be pointing at you. I was just thinking about these guys who live for Satan seven days a week."

"But," Danny put in, turning to Kit, "the Bible tells us that it doesn't make any difference whether our sins are big or little, or whether they are few or many. The important thing is whether or not we have accepted the Lord Jesus Christ as our personal Savior. If we haven't done that, we're lost, regardless of how good we have been living."

48

Kit colored slightly and turned away. The boys were standing in the old building with their backs toward the door. Suddenly there was a harsh, strident voice behind them.

"Stick 'em up! Stick 'em up and keep 'em up!"

SIX
A strange prospector

"Thought you could fool old Jim Harrison and get away with it did you?" the voice demanded triumphantly. "Well, there ain't nobody in these here hills can do that. And don't you ever forget it."

Danny Orlis turned his head slightly, his heart hammering in his throat. Behind them stood a squat, gray-bearded old fellow in tattered clothes, his hat pushed back on his bushy white hair and his hands fondling a heavy rifle, which, at the moment, was pointed at the floor.

"Now, young man!" Jim Harrison ordered gruffly as he raised the rifle significantly. "Don't you try any funny stuff. You stay turned around until I tell you different. And keep them hands up high. I might be old, but I ain't rusty with this here shooting iron."

"But what's wrong?" questioned Larry. "What have we done?"

"Don't give me that," the old prospector retorted, turning a little to spit contemptuously on the floor. "You know that it ain't what you done that's got me riled up. It's what you're aimin' to do."

He turned to Kit. "You in the heavy jacket, turn around real slow and easy. And keep them hands up."

Kit did as he was told. When Kit had turned, Jim Harrison had Larry turn, and, then Danny.

"Now, all three of you, just stand right where you are, and don't give me no trouble." He chuckled mirthlessly. "So you thought you could slip up here and run the line for that there highway without having to reckon with Jim Harrison? Well, you got fooled!"

"We don't know what you're talking about," Kit put in. "We didn't come up here to do any surveying for a highway. We just came up on a little trip to look at some—to look at some . . ." His voice trailed away as Danny looked at him sharply and shook his head.

"Now, listen here, young man," the old fellow retorted, his voice rising, "don't you lie to Jim Harrison. I wrote to them fellers back in Washington. Told 'em what was going to happen if they tried to put that there road through these parts."

He turned to spit again.

"A highway! If I let 'em put through that highway, like they figured on doing, the first thing you know, this whole country would be littered with filling stations and beer bottles, and little sleeping houses. A body won't have no rest at all. No, sir, I've made up my mind. I ain't going to let 'em do it!"

"But what Kit said is true," Danny told him seriously. "We don't have anything to do with that highway. We don't even know where it's going to be. We just came up to look around."

"That's what they all say." He had lowered his rifle a little while he talked with them. Suddenly he raised

51

it. "The last fellers came up to go fishing, they told me. I even took 'em back to my own favorite trout stream. But did they appreciate it? Soon as my back was turned, they put up their little instruments and started looking through 'em. You can just bet your last dollar that I took care of them fellers, the same way I'm fixin' to take care of you."

Kit Carson looked at Danny and made a significant motion toward his head with his finger. Danny nodded in complete agreement.

"Now, keep them hands up!"

"You—you don't need to hold that gun on us," Larry stammered. "We're not going to put our hands down or—or give you any trouble."

"You can just bet your sweet life you're not, young man." He motioned toward the door with the barrel of his gun. "Come on, now. Get your horses watered and hobbled and turned out to grass. You're going to stay right here with me tonight."

"B–b–but what are you going to do with us?" Kit asked, his voice trembling a little.

"Never you mind about that, Buster. You just take good care that you don't make me no madder than I am. That's what you've got to do."

Old Jim Harrison herded the boys out of the abandoned saloon ahead of him and, brandishing his rifle, made them take their horses out behind the hotel to water them at the little stream which ran just below the ghost town. Then he ordered them to hobble their mounts and pack animals and turn them loose on the grass.

"Now, come on!" he ordered harshly. "Get in that hotel, and be quick about it."

52

Danny lagged a little, and the old prospector prodded him in the back with the rifle.

"Don't try any funny stuff, Buster. I'm right behind you."

He directed the three boys into the hotel lobby, where he made them sit in one corner on the floor. Danny saw at a glance that there were no doors or windows close to them. Old Jim Harrison planted himself in front of the ancient clerk's desk, sitting on the floor and facing them. He laid his gun significantly close to his hands, across his knees.

"Now, I warned you before, and I'm warning you again," he exclaimed, scowling fiercely, "the safety's off, and this here rifle's loaded, and I'm ready for anything. So don't you fellers start anything less you figure you can finish it."

"No," Kit put in, "we aren't going to cause you any trouble."

"You won't be causing me no trouble, Buster." He patted his battered old rifle with his gnarled, bony hand. "No trouble at all."

Danny poked Kit with his elbow and signaled for him to be quiet. For half an hour nobody said a word. The old man watched them, his eagle-sharp eyes never leaving their faces. But after a time he began to nod a little, and his eyelids drooped almost imperceptibly.

Kit turned and whispered to Danny, "I think he's going to sleep."

Danny nodded and put a warning finger to his lips. Another half an hour passed, and old Jim Harrison's chin dropped until it was resting on his dirty Mackinaw.

"Do you think we can rush him?" Larry whispered, leaning over so that both Kit and Danny could hear what he had to say.

"I was just wondering about that myself," Danny answered. "If we can slip close enough to him so that we can jump him before he gets that rifle up, we'll be all right."

"The trouble is that he has that old cannon loaded," Kit protested hoarsely, "and he's just nutty enough to use it if he wakes up before we get to him."

"That's a chance we'll have to take," Danny whispered to his companions. "We have to get out of here. Every minute counts if we're going to find out what Harold's up to and why he threatened us if we didn't leave town this morning."

Larry shuddered.

"I never saw anyone like you, Danny," he said tensely. "Here we are, sitting in an abandoned hotel in a ghost town, with a lunatic prospector holding us captive, and you start worrying about how we can get away from him. And why? So we can get mixed up with another guy who's threatened us unless we go back to Iron Mountain pronto."

Danny and Kit both grinned a little at their companion. "Let's see if we can slip a little closer to him," Danny said, "and when I count three, we'll all jump him at once."

"OK," Kit agreed under his breath. "But when we do it, I sure hope he doesn't have that gun of his pointed at me. I have a hunch that the old boy isn't as sound asleep as we'd like to think he is."

Larry looked quickly at the man with the rifle and scooted forward slightly. Kit moved alongside him, inching so slowly and quietly that, had old Jim Harrison been watching him, he might have missed seeing it.

The two boys looked back at Danny. It was his turn to move. Before he did so, he bowed his head and began to pray silently.

"Heavenly Father," he prayed, scarcely moving his lips, "be with us, and guide us, and help us now to get away from Mr. Harrison. Help us to reach him before he wakes up, and—and Lord Jesus, we pray that nobody will be hurt, especially not Mr. Harrison." Danny prayed for Kit's salvation, too, and for help in finding out about the twins' land.

"And through it all," he concluded, "we pray that thy will might be done and thy name glorified. . . ."

When he had finished praying, he looked up to see that Larry also had his head bowed and was praying. Kit had been watching both of them. There was a queer, quizzical look on his face as his gaze met Danny's.

"All ready?" Danny whispered when he had slid up even with his companions.

Larry nodded tensely.

"OK," Kit answered, clenching his fists and tightening his muscles like the spring on a trap.

"One—two—three!"

As Danny whispered, "Three!" the boys crouched and would have sprung on the old prospector, but his head popped up. He snapped the rifle to his shoulders.

"Now, now, now! I told you not to try any funny stuff, didn't I? Thought old Jim was asleep, didn't you? Thought you were going to get over here and take this rifle away, didn't you?" He paused momentarily, his faded blue eyes narrowing.

"Well, I can tell you one thing—this old prospector has tangled with fellers a lot tougher than the three of you, and he's took care of 'em, too!"

He stared hard at Larry, then at Kit, finally at Danny. "Now, I don't want to have to warn you again," he snarled. "Just sit back down there and go to sleep! The next time I won't be so easy with you!"

SEVEN
Three prisoners

Old Jim Harrison did not take his eyes off the boys
for an instant the rest of the night. His trigger hand
rested on the stock of the rifle, and his whole body
seemed poised in tense expectation, as though he half
hoped that they would try to make a break for it.

"You young fellers had just as well quit watching
me and lay down and go to sleep," he rasped. "You
ain't going to get away with double-dealing old Jim. If
you know what's good for you, you won't even try it."
He turned to Danny. "And that goes for you, too,
Buster. Don't you forget it."

For several minutes the boys looked at one another
and their captor.

"I think we might just as well go to sleep, guys,"
Danny said, leaning back against the wall and closing
his eyes.

"Now, that's more like it," Jim Harrison barked.

Larry straightened out his leg, scraping his heel on
the floor. Instantly the rifle came up.

"I wouldn't try that, Buster," he said ominously.

"Just lay back down there and go to sleep. Ain't no sense in all of you being awake, just because I got to be."

For half an hour or more Danny Orlis feigned sleep, breathing with studied regularity and keeping his eyes tightly closed. Finally he opened them slightly to see whether or not the old prospector had started to nod again.

The boys' attempted escape had alerted their self-styled jailer. Old Jim did not move or close his eyes all night long. Every time Danny squinted at him, he was staring from one of his captives to another, his hand never leaving its place on the rifle, a scant inch from the trigger.

Danny dozed fitfully, despite the fact that they were being held prisoners. He dozed because he could stay awake no longer. But every now and then he would stir slightly and open his eyes just a crack to watch the old prospector. Larry and Kit must have been doing the same. Once when Danny awoke and glanced quickly about, he saw that Larry's friend was eyeing him.

Finally the long night passed, and the dust-laden hotel was faintly lighted with the first gray streaks of dawn. The smoky kerosene lamp seemed even more feeble than ever as the light of day began to chase away the darkness. Danny opened his eyes and stretched wearily.

With the coming of morning the old prospector stirred.

"Well," he said, getting stiffly to his feet and cradling his rifle in his arms, "we'd just as well go into the kitchen and fix some breakfast. If you fellers want anything to eat, you're going to have to cook it."

He prodded them into the kitchen in the back of the hotel building and waved Danny to the stove.

"You look like you can cook, Buster," he ordered. "Get that stove to going, and fry us some bacon and eggs." With his left hand he reached out and dipped a drink of water from the pail on the washstand. All the while his sharp gaze never left the boys. When he finished drinking, he said to Larry, "Better set that table. We've got us a lot to do today."

Danny and Larry quickly did as they were told. Jim Harrison was in no mood for trifling. Kit helped build a fire in the stove, and in a few minutes the water for the coffee was boiling.

"I wrote to them fellers back in Washington about that highway they've been fixin' to put in here," Jim continued, more to himself than to the boys. "I warned 'em what was going to happen if they didn't forget about it. But it looks like they wouldn't listen to me. Now they'll have to suffer for it."

"W—what are you planning on doing?" Kit asked, trying to sound casual as he eyed the old prospector.

"Never you mind, Buster. Never you mind about that. You'll find out soon enough."

When Danny had finished cooking breakfast and they had sat down at the table to eat, Danny and Larry bowed their heads and prayed silently.

"Now what did you go and do that for?" Jim asked suspiciously. "What's going on here?"

Danny looked up at him. "We were asking God's blessing on the food," he explained.

Old Jim Harrison squinted one eye and looked at him questioningly. "What do you mean by that?"

"Larry and I are Christians," Danny answered, putting down his fork and turning in his chair until he faced the prospector. "We've put our trust in the Lord Jesus Christ and are trying to live the way he wants us to live."

Jim grunted his disapproval. "What's that got to do with this—this bowing over victuals?" he demanded.

"It has everything to do with it," Danny told him. "God has made everything, Mr. Harrison. He made these hills you love so much, and the deer and elk, and the trout streams—everything. And he gave them to us to use as we have need. That's why we thank him at mealtime."

The old prospector leaned forward intently.

"Don't rightly know that I ever heard anything like that before," he said at last. Suddenly a faraway look came into his eyes. "I've done a sight of pondering, though, up here in the hills alone, when I look down over the valley, lying asleep in the soft light of the summer moon, or when I see a doe suckling her fawn."

"And another thing he's done," Danny went on seriously, "is to provide a Savior for us. He sent the Lord Jesus Christ into the world to die on the cross and to be raised again, so that you and I and everybody who confesses his sins and puts his trust in Christ might be saved."

Jim Harrison looked at him blankly, as though Danny had suddenly begun to speak some strange language which he had never heard before.

"That's right," Danny's cousin put in. "God sent his Son so that we could be saved. I can tell you, Jim, that it's a wonderful thing to put your trust in Christ and accept the salvation he offers."

"It doesn't matter whether we're young or old, or what we've done," Danny continued. "If we just confess that we are sinners and need a Savior, and if we put our trust in Christ, we can know that we are Christians. That's the only way we can have eternal life."

Kit Carson coughed nervously, and Danny turned for an instant to stare at him. Larry's tall, lanky friend was twisting nervously. His face had become white, and he was staring at his plate.

Old Jim Harrison's hand wandered from the trigger of his rifle.

"I reckon it's too late for an old feller like me to be thinking about anything like that," he said after a time. "If I was the age of this young feller, it might be. . . ." The words trailed away dismally.

Danny thought he detected a strange, wistful note in the old prospector's voice; but if he had, it was gone in an instant. Jim Harrison pushed back from the table and got noisily to his feet, raising his rifle menacingly.

"We been sittin' here too long now," he snarled, motioning with the barrel of his rifle. "Come on."

The three boys looked at one another desperately. There was a queer, almost violent look in the old man's eyes, and his finger was disconcertingly close to the trigger as he ushered Danny and the others ahead of him out of the dilapidated old hotel.

"Get on down the road there, and be quick about it," he ordered, prodding Kit with his gun. "I ain't got all day."

"Shall we try rushing him, Kit?" Danny muttered under his breath as he and Larry's friend went out the door.

"We've got to have a chance first," Kit whispered back.

Two or three times as they walked down the dusty, winding street of the deserted ghost town, Danny cast quick, sidelong glances over his shoulder, mentally calculating the distance back to where Jim Harrison was, trying to weigh his chances of reaching the prospector before he could fire. But there would be no chance. Jim stayed behind them just far enough so that they could not whirl and jerk the rifle from him.

Danny's heart was hammering a loud tattoo, and his hands were trembling as he brushed the cold sweat from his forehead.

Jim Harrison was striding jauntily behind them, his keen blue eyes still alight with anger. His battered old hat was set on his shaggy white hair at a rakish angle, and he wiped at his bearded mouth with a dirty sleeve as he hurried the boys on ahead of him.

At the edge of town he stopped.

"I'm aimin' to do something I hadn't ought to do," he growled. "I'm going to send you young fellers on about your business." He turned and spat into the dust at his feet. "But you've got to do what old Jim Harrison tells you."

"Oh, you won't need to worry about that," Kit assured him.

"It ain't you I'm worried about, Buster," Jim retorted. "It's him." He jerked his head toward Danny. "I want you fellers to start marching down this here trail toward Scranton, and I don't want you to stop until you get there. And when you get to a telephone, you can call that boss of yours in Washington and tell him old Jim Harrison did what he said he would. He run you out of the mountains, and he's going to run every last livin' feller that comes in here to try and put through that road."

He stopped for a moment, breathing heavily. "You tell him that if they're figgerin' on building that there road, they'd better send the militia up here first. They're going to need 'em!"

"Do you mean you're going to let us go?" Larry asked, as though he could scarcely believe what he had heard.

"That's what I aim to do, Buster," the old prospector went on. "That is, I aim to do it if you don't rile me up and get me mad." He kicked a small pebble with his toe. "You just start right down that trail, fellers, and keep going. I'll be watching, so don't try any funny stuff."

"But what about our horses?" Danny put in. Without them there would be no chance of finding the tract of Bauer land which he had come all the way from Angle Inlet to investigate.

"Don't you worry about the horses," Jim Harrison told him. "If you keep on going, like you're supposed to, and don't cause me no trouble, I'll turn them critters loose after a while." He wiped at his mouth again with a grimy sleeve. There's one thing nobody can say about old Jim Harrison. He never stole anything. You just keep on about your business, and I'll turn them horses loose. They'll probably beat you back to the ranch where you hired 'em. They know their way home a sight better than you do."

Danny started to speak, but Kit took his arm.

"Come on," he muttered under his breath. "Quit pressing our luck. He's letting us go. Let's be on our way while he's still in a good mood."

"Right smart idea," the old prospector grunted.

Without a backward glance Larry started down the trail toward Scranton. Kit ran after him, but Danny turned to face the old prospector.

"I wish you'd think about this matter of becoming a Christian, Mr. Harrison," he said seriously. "It's really wonderful to know that you're going to heaven when you die and that the sins you've committed aren't going to keep you from eternal life with the Lord Jesus."

The prospector's face clouded, and he raised the gun slightly. "Never you mind about me, young feller," he snarled. "I'll look after myself. Get on down that trail before I change my mind."

Danny looked at him for a moment. Then he turned and hurried to catch up with his companions.

"Man!" Kit exclaimed, wiping his sweat-covered forehead and sighing deeply in relief. "If we ever talked to a guy who was ready for the asylum, old Jim is. He's crazy as a loon."

"I really thought he was going to take a shot at us when he led us out on the edge of town like this," Larry said, his voice still trembling.

But Danny scarcely heard them.

"I don't know about that," he said. "Jim Harrison is sort of queer—but, like Dad says about some of the guys up our way, his real need is for the Lord Jesus Christ as his personal Savior."

EIGHT
A daring recovery

Larry Anders was two steps ahead of Danny and Kit, almost running down the trail.

"I'm mighty glad to be away from old Mr. Harrison, anyway," he panted over his shoulder, "and out of that ghost town. He might not have seemed crazy to you, Danny, but he acted plenty buggy to me."

"You said it!" Kit replied. "If I never see him again, it'll be too soon." He looked over at Danny. "If you're going back to finish trying to convert him, you'll have to go without me."

"I don't plan on doing that right now," Danny laughed, "but I do hate to go back without those horses."

They had rounded several bends in the narrow, twisting trail and were shielded from Jim Harrison's view. As soon as Danny saw that, he stopped. His companions did likewise.

"Those horses are the least of my worries," Kit retorted, laughing. "I'm not even going to complain about the sore feet we'll have when we finally get back to Scranton."

"It isn't only the horses," Danny continued. "There's Harold. We still haven't found out why he's here at Scranton and why he threatened us if we didn't go back to Iron Mountain. And we don't know anything at all about the land the twins own. What's more, we can't find out anything about it if we don't get our horses and our supplies."

Kit, who had sat down on a big rock and was whittling absentmindedly with his jackknife, looked up.

"You aren't suggesting that we go back up there and try to take our horses away from old Jim, are you?" he asked, his voice plainly revealing that he thought Danny was as crazy as Jim for even having such an idea.

"I don't know what I'm suggesting," Danny answered.

"I've just been thinking," Kit said, "that time must mean a lot in this deal with Harold. He knows that he can't get hold of the land legally, so there isn't any use in his trying to keep you away from it for that reason. There must be some special reason why he doesn't want us to be over on the twins' land at this particular time."

Danny wrinkled his forehead. "I'd never thought of that," he said staring out across the valley at the little town of Scranton, which lay halfway up the range, across the river. "But I can't see how that would make any difference. Why would it be important for him to keep us out of there now but not later?"

Kit looked up at him and grinned. "That's for you to figure out."

"To tell the truth," Larry said, shivering, "I haven't thought of a thing except that old man up there with the rifle. I could almost feel that bullet go slamming into my back when we left there a little while ago. That's as close a call as any of us have ever had."

There was a short silence.

"Unless we get those horses from Harrison, we're going to lose two whole days in going up to the Bauer land," Danny said thoughtfully. "We might lose even more. The ranch might refuse to let us have any more horses if we come back without the ones we're supposed to have now."

"I'll take my chances on that," Larry said quickly.

"It could mean that we'd miss finding out about the land altogether. The more I think about what Kit said, the more it makes sense. I don't know how it could make any difference to have us out of the way right now, but I'm convinced that it does."

Kit Carson nodded seriously. "I was just wondering, Danny. Do you suppose we even have a chance of getting those horses back from him—without risking our necks, I mean?"

Larry shook his head. "If he ever caught us up there snooping around, he'd use that old blunderbuss he kept pointed at us."

"Just the same," Danny went on, "it's the only thing we can do. Somehow we'll have to get those horses and go over that tract of land from one end to the other before Harold does whatever he's planning to do."

"Horses that are hobbled do stray around a little," Larry said when he saw that Danny was serious about getting their mounts back. "If we can slip back to where they're grazing, we can wait there until they're out of Mr. Harrison's sight. Then we can slip down and grab them before he knows it."

"I thought you were scared," Kit put in.

"I am," Larry told him, grinning crookedly. "That's why I decided to figure out a way to take our horses without being caught."

"Well, come on," Kit said, putting his knife away. "If you guys are bound and determined to get yourselves into real trouble, I'll just have to go along with you."

They had started back up the trail in the direction from which they had come a moment or two before, when Larry stopped.

"You know, guys," he said softly, "we're forgetting something."

"What's that?"

"We haven't asked for the Lord's guidance." With that he and Danny bowed their heads. "Our Father and our God," Larry prayed intently, "we thank you for helping us to be released by Jim Harrison. Now we pray that you will be with us while we go back for our horses. Help us to keep out of the prospector's sight and get the horses and our supplies without trouble. And help us to find out the mystery of the Bauer land before it's too late."

When he had finished praying, Danny followed suit. Then they started out again. With Danny in the lead, they left the trail and made their way stealthily up into the woods, some two or three hundred yards, to a place where they would not be seen by anyone who happened to be watching the trail. Then Danny began to move cautiously toward the ghost town.

"There's one thing I must say about you guys and your praying," Kit remarked, after a time. "You certainly go about it as though it does some good."

"It does," Danny told him. "We have Christ's assurance that he does hear and answer the prayers of believers."

Kit looked at him queerily and started on again. For several minutes no one spoke.

"Stay down," Danny whispered, "and don't make any noise. That old guy's eyes and ears are as sharp as an elk's."

"Don't worry," Kit whispered back. "Nobody's going to see or hear me!"

Slowly, carefully, they made their way through the pine trees toward the ghost town. They had walked farther down the trail than they had supposed, and now, as they were making their way cautiously back, each step seemed a mile. Danny looked at his watch. They had been moving for twenty minutes. That ought to bring them close. He turned and put a warning finger to his lips. From somewhere just below them he could hear a horse whinny.

"Psst!" Larry whispered hoarsely. "They're right down there!"

"Take it easy," Danny cautioned. "We can't have anything go wrong now!"

For a moment or two they froze where they were standing. Then Danny signaled to the boys behind him, and they began to move cautiously down toward their horses.

Danny could feel his heart hammering against his

ribs. His stomach was like a ball of ice, and his tongue was thick and dry. He moistened his lips nervously and wiped at the sweat on his face with the back of his trembling hand.

"Remember," Danny instructed in a hoarse whisper, "we've got to have those pack horses, too—and our grub and sleeping bags, if possible."

"Listen," Larry countered, "all I agreed to do was to come back here and help get our saddle horses. I didn't hear anybody say a word about those mules. What's old Jim supposed to be doing while we take the hobbles off five animals, after we've loaded the pack saddles of two of them?"

"We kept him up all night," Kit said in an undertone. "Maybe he's at home in bed."

"We won't have any such luck," Larry told him. "He's probably sitting right down there with those horses now, with his cannon on his lap, just waiting for us."

Nevertheless, when they started down through the trees to the place where the horses and pack mules were grazing, Larry was in the lead. They had been moving higher above the trail as they neared the ghost town, and again they found that they had farther to go than they had supposed.

At last Danny stopped. "They're right below us," he whispered, his voice as taut as a string on a violin. "Let's move down a little closer and get ready before we make a run for it."

"Don't you think one of us ought to slip down as close as he can and see if old Jim does happen to be around anywhere?" Kit asked. "He's not as apt to see or hear one of us as he is all three."

"I think you've got something there," Danny answered, nodding.

Cautiously he began to edge forward. He had not realized it before, but now he saw that they were some thirty or forty feet above the little patch of grassland which Jim Harrison called his pasture. That meant that they would have to scramble down among the rocks, making perfect targets for the aged prospector if he happened to spot them.

Danny looked up and down the low cliff. It ran as far as he could see in either direction. He remembered now that it stretched for a mile or more up the mountain. This still was the best approach. He took a deep breath and wriggled closer to the rim of the cliff. He could see the two pack mules, grazing peacefully, and nearby was Larry's saddle horse and the one that Kit had been riding.

At that instant a rifle shot exploded with breath-snatching suddenness below them, and they heard the bullet whistle over their heads.

"All right, Buster!" Jim Harrison shouted. "I warned you! I told you what would happen!"

Danny flattened himself against the rocks, burying his head in his arms.

"I warned you about what would happen if you came back here! Now, get going before I lose my temper!"

Panting, Danny wriggled backward to the place where his companions were crouched.

"How do you suppose he saw you?" Larry demanded in a hoarse whisper.

"I told you that guy has eyes like an eagle," Danny retorted.

"I was taking the hobbles off of these horses," Harrison shouted up to Danny, "just like I said I would. But I ain't going to do it now! I'm going to put them hobbles back, and I'll keep 'em on until I know you fellers are plumb out of the country!"

With that the old prospector grasped the horse that Danny had been riding and bent down to snap the hobbles back into place. He tried to accomplish the task without laying down his gun, and he fumbled a little with the snap.

With a quick motion Kit scooped up a small rock and threw it at the horse, shouting at the same time.

The rock thumped the wiry little pinto on the hip. She squealed with fright and reared.

In his scramble to get out of the way, old Jim Harrison dropped his rifle. The horse bumped him with her shoulder, and he crumpled to the ground.

NINE
A sprained ankle

Old Jim Harrison groaned weakly and rolled over, struggling to get to his feet.

"Just a minute, Mr. Harrison!" Danny called out to the injured man, who was lying helpless on the ground below them. "We'll be right down."

He took a step or two toward the edge of the low cliff, but Kit grasped him by the arm.

"You aren't going down there, are you?" Kit Carson demanded. "He might still have a gun on him, or crawl over to the one he did have. And if he does, there's no telling what he'll do."

Larry made a move to follow his cousin, but he stopped uncertainly beside Danny and Kit.

"We can't leave him lying down there," Danny protested. "He's badly hurt. We'll have to help him."

"He wouldn't have given us any help if we'd been in that fix," Kit retorted, a trace of bitterness in his voice. "That's my motto—treat people just the way they treat you."

"We can't do that," Danny said. "He's old and helpless, and he's hurt. We'll have to go down and do what we can for him."

Reluctantly Kit relaxed his grip on Danny's arm. Danny hurried down the moss-covered granite cliff and ran to the place where old Jim Harrison was lying. Kit and Larry were close behind him.

"What are you going to do?" Harrison demanded, his high-pitched voice quivering with fright. "What are you going to do to me?"

The old prospector looked wildly about, searching desperately for some means of escape. He reminded Danny of a fawn that one of the guys up on the Angle had caught after some outside hunter had killed its mother. It had that same bewildered, terror-stricken look in its eyes.

"I didn't mean it, fellers," he continued, pleading. "I wouldn't have hurt you. I—I could have shot you all a little while ago, but I just wanted to scare you away. Honest, fellers."

"Let me take a look at that ankle, Mr. Harrison," Danny said softly as he knelt beside the prospector. "You might have broken it, falling so hard."

"Don't mind me, Buster," Jim repeated. "You just take your horses and go on about your business. Just—" He turned quickly and looked in desperation toward his rifle, which was lying several paces away.

"We'll have to hurry and take this boot off before his ankle swells too badly," Danny said to his companions, "or we might have to cut it. Kit, would you help me with this, please?"

Kit looked at the drawn, bearded face of the old prospector and squatted down beside Danny to help him remove the boot. Harrison stifled a quick cry of pain as

Danny loosened the bootlace and Kit pulled off the boot.

"Say," Danny exclaimed, looking at the swollen ankle, "that's bad. You have a terrible sprain here, and your ankle might be broken."

"We'd better carry him back to the hotel," Larry said. "We'll have to put some cold packs on that ankle as soon as we can."

"We ought to be thinking about getting over to that Bauer land," Kit put in. "Every second counts in that deal."

"The main thing right now," Danny said, "is for us to move Mr. Harrison back to the hotel and begin to treat his ankle."

"You don't need to worry about me, fellers," the old prospector put in hurriedly, gritting his teeth to keep the boys from seeing how much pain he was in. "You just go about your business. I'll be all right."

"We aren't going to leave," Danny told him, "until we know that you're safe in the hotel and that your ankle is getting well."

Old Jim Harrison looked at him queerly. "You mean that, don't you?" he asked, as though he could scarcely believe it, even yet. "You ain't going to hurt an old man."

The boys picked him up, remarking at how light he was, and carried him back to the dingy, dirt-ridden hotel.

"Why don't you put him on the bed?" Danny suggested, turning toward the door. "I'll go out to the stream and get some cold water."

In ten or fifteen minutes the boys had old Mr. Harrison undressed and in bed, with a cold compress on his injured ankle.

"Does it feel any better now?" Danny asked him.

He nodded slightly and managed a queer little smile. "I never did have anybody treat me like you fellers have."

"If you'll tell us where your food is now, Mr. Harrison," Larry said, "we'll see if we can fix you something to eat before we leave."

"Do you think we'll be able to leave him?" Danny asked softly. "We still don't know anything about that ankle. It might be hurt worse than we think."

He had not intended for the old prospector to hear him, but as he spoke, Harrison turned to face him.

"You boys won't need to worry about me," he said. "I feel a lot better already. I'll be all right."

Danny motioned to his companions, and they all went outside the old prospector's room and closed the door.

"What do you think?" he asked Larry and Kit.

"I don't know," Larry said. "He seems to be feeling better now. Do you suppose that ankle of his is broken?"

Danny shook his head. "I don't think so," he said. "I've seen quite a few broken ankles, but this looks more like a sprain to me. It must be a bad one, though."

"I think he'll be OK," Kit put in. "If his ankle is just sprained, he ought to be able to hobble around a little."

"We can bring in plenty of wood and water and leave enough food out where he can reach it so that he can cook a little for himself. I'm sure he'll be all right."

"Well," Danny answered, "we can see how he is after

he eats. If he's going to be all right, maybe we should go on down to Scranton. I've just been thinking. Harold warned me to leave town. Maybe the answer to this whole thing is down there. Perhaps we've been going at it backwards."

"I'd never thought of that," Kit echoed. "We've been wasting our time up here if that's true. But I don't see why it would hurt for us to leave the old man here alone. After all, he wasn't thinking so much of us when he took us out to the edge of town and told us that we'd have to walk back to Scranton."

"I know that," Danny replied, "but he needs help now. It wouldn't be Christian for us to go away and leave him."

Kit looked at him quizzically. "You know," he said, "I can't figure you two out. This business of talking religion is one thing, but you two guys act as though you try to live up to it."

"That's exactly right, Kit," Danny told him. "I know we both do an awfully poor job of it, but we do try to live the way we feel the Lord wants us to live. So, you see, we just can't go away and leave Mr. Harrison as long as he really needs us."

Kit Carson shook his head.

TEN
A new beginning

When Danny and his companions came back into the old prospector's room, he had pulled himself up in bed.

"That ankle feels a lot better now," he said to Danny. "You fixed it up like you knew how."

Danny smiled. "I've helped my mother with some ankles like yours," he said, "and I've watched her take care of a good many others. You see, up where we live there aren't any doctors, so we have to take care of such things ourselves."

Danny would have turned to his companions, but the bewhiskered, wizened old man reached out and grasped his arm with fingers of steel.

"Just a minute, Buster," he said. "I've got some talking to do with you."

Danny pulled up a backless chair and sat down beside the bed.

"Sure thing," he said.

There was a long silence. Finally the old man relaxed his grip.

"Why did you do it?" he asked. "Why did you boys

stay here and look after me this way, when you know how terrible I treated you?"

"It's like I tried to tell you," Danny said softly. "Larry and I are Christians. We have put our trust in the Lord Jesus, and we're trying to live the way he wants us to live. We knew that he would never have left you lying there on the ground without any help."

Old Jim Harrison pursed his bearded lips thoughtfully.

"I never had anyone treat me like that before," he said. "Makes a feller . . ." His voice trailed away.

Danny sat there silently for a moment or two.

"I certainly wish you'd accept the Lord Jesus Christ as your Savior, Mr. Harrison."

Larry came in with a pail of cold water just then, and Danny changed the compress on the prospector's ankle. It looked as though the swelling might be going down a little. At least it was not any worse.

"You need the Lord Jesus," Danny continued.

For an instant Harrison's watery blue eyes saddened noticeably. "He wouldn't be interested in an old man like me," he said. "Not one who's done the things I've done."

"Oh, but he is," Danny assured him quickly. "It doesn't make any difference whether we're young or old, whether we've sinned a lot or just a little—we're all lost and headed for an eternity without the Lord if we haven't accepted him as our Savior. If we have confessed our sins and put our trust in him, then we are saved. God doesn't pay any attention to our age, or what we've done, or anything else, as long as we meet the conditions which he has set down for salvation."

Danny had forgotten that his companions were in

the room with him until Kit coughed nervously. Walking over to the grimy window, he suddenly became engrossed in something outside.

"Is—is that the truth?" Harrison demanded.

"That's what the Bible says," Danny told him. "If I were saying this, it could be wrong. I could make a mistake. But the Bible is the Word of God."

"I—I don't know much about this business," Mr. Harrison began uncertainly, his voice quivering with emotion. "But I know this much—I never met anybody before who treated me the way you fellers did. You make me feel ashamed of myself, like I'm carrying a load of sin around with me. I—I don't know just how to go about it, but I want to be like you. You'll help me, won't you?" He took hold of Danny's arm again, squeezing it with his bony fingers.

Danny Orlis knelt beside the old prospector's bed and guided him haltingly through a prayer of confession. When he finished, Danny prayed, asking God to watch over Mr. Harrison and help him to understand more of the Scriptures and what accepting Christ as his Savior really meant.

Danny talked to him about the Lord Jesus, explaining again and again the way of salvation, so that the old fellow would be absolutely sure of the step which he had taken. Danny even took out his Testament and laid it on the wobbly little table beside the bed.

"You read this every day, Mr. Harrison," he said. "A Christian ought to read God's Word so that he'll know about Jesus and how he wants him to live."

Kit, who had been nervously pacing the floor while Danny was talking and praying with the old prospector, came over to Danny.

"Danny," he said, "why don't we move Mr. Harrison's bed out in one corner of the kitchen? Then he won't have to worry about getting around."

"You don't have to worry about me," Harrison protested again. This time there was a new tone in his voice. "I'll get along all right."

"Are you sure?" Danny asked again.

"I been taking care of myself for nigh onto seventy years," he informed him. "Reckon I can keep on doing it."

"We wouldn't think of leaving you if it weren't for this land that we're supposed to look at."

"What land is that you're talking about?" Jim Harrison put in quickly. "I've been living in these parts all my life. There ain't very much around these hills that I don't know about."

"I never thought that you might be able to help us," Danny said hurriedly. "We want to check that tract of land that belongs to the Bauer estate. We thought maybe the highway was going through there, or something, to make it valuable. There's a fellow who has been doing his best to get hold of it, and we don't know why."

"Know all about it," the old prospector said gruffly. "Land used to be owned by a good friend of mine, name of John Bauer. Him and me did a lot of prospecting over there along the ridge. Got a mighty good trout stream on his land, I can tell you that much."

"But how about the highway?" Danny asked him. "Will it go close?"

Harrison shook his head. "No," he said finally. "Won't go closer than fifteen or twenty miles."

81

"Then why would this Harold try so hard to get it?" Danny asked. "And why would he try to keep us from even seeing the place?"

"Can't rightly answer that," Harrison said. "But I got a good idea. Yes, sir, I got a good idea."

The boys leaned forward tensely. Something about the old man's manner set their hearts to racing.

"What is it?" Larry asked.

"It's because of them rocks that talk!"

ELEVEN
Dangerous trail

A blank look appeared on Danny Orlis' face.

"The rocks that talk?" he echoed. "What do you mean by that?"

Old Jim Harrison grinned up at him. "That's just what I call 'em—the rocks that talk. It's that there new stuff, that uranium, or whatever it is."

"Uranium!" the boys shouted in unison. "Are you sure?"

"Yes, sir," the old prospector answered. "Old John Bauer and me, we scratched up and down that ridge for fifteen years together and never found anything more valuable than quartz and granite. Then this here Harold guy comes up and stumbles onto uranium, the first thing."

Danny stared at his companions.

"That explains everything," he said. "That explains why Harold has been so anxious to get hold of that stretch of land. He wanted to have control of it so he would have the uranium mine."

"Uranium!" Kit repeated. "And here we were thinking it was a little thing like that highway they're going to build."

"No wonder Harold has been so desperate," Larry put in.

"Yes, sir," old Jim Harrison went on, "I was in town just the other day to get some grub and supplies for winter, and the county clerk told me about it. He said my old sidekick's youngest boy had made a rich strike of uranium over on the ridge, and he had a chance to be cut in on it."

"The county clerk had a chance to get a cut!" Danny repeated. "That explains something else. That tells us why he gave us a bum steer when we asked about going out to the Bauer land. Harold probably told him that he would give him a share in it if he would keep us from finding it."

"That makes sense," Larry said, "but I still can't understand why he would be so anxious to keep us away from the land, anyway. It doesn't belong to him. Sooner or later your dad would have found out about the uranium strike and could have taken it away from him."

"Maybe it's such a rich strike he can make a fortune for himself in just a little while," Kit Carson put in. "If he could keep you from finding out about it, Danny, he would have a chance to work the mine until he had all the money he'd ever need."

Danny nodded, drawing his mouth into a thin, hard line. "That means that we'll have to go over there just as fast as we can," he said determinedly. "If there's uranium there, we've got to find out about it so we can keep Harold from working it."

"How'll we find out if there is uranium on the ridge unless we go back to Scranton and pick up a scintillator or a Geiger counter?" Kit asked. "I don't think there's any other way of knowing whether or not you've found the stuff. You could be sitting on a mountain of it and never know the difference."

"You don't give me credit for nothing, fellers." The old prospector laughed heartily. "Everyone in the hills has got one of them things now. I've stuck that little box of mine on so many rocks that I've been seeing rocks in my sleep, especially after that feller down in Scranton told me about what happened over on the ridge."

"You mean that you've got a Geiger counter here?" Danny asked, surprised.

"Yes, sirree. I'm going to make a strike one of these days, that's what I'm going to do." For an instant a vacant stare came into the man's eyes as he thought of all the years he had been searching for his strike, first in gold or silver or copper and now in the magical uranium.

"Excuse me, fellers," he said suddenly. "It's right in that little closet under the stairs. You can use it if you want to."

"Say, that'll be great," Danny replied. "We'll bring it back to you when we've finished with it."

"I ain't worried about that. Not worried at all." He wiped his mouth with the back of his hand. "Bring the thing in here, and I'll show you how she works."

Larry ran for the Geiger counter, and the old prospector explained to them how to use it.

"Ain't nothing to it," he concluded. "You just move

the thing close to the rocks, and if there's any of that there uranium anywhere close, the little box starts to talk—tick, tick, tick."

Danny examined the Geiger counter carefully and put it back in its leather case. "You've saved us a long trip back to Scranton for one of these things, Mr. Harrison. We surely do appreciate it."

"You've saved me a sight more than that," Jim said, his eyes growing misty. "Just think! I'd have lived up here and died without ever knowing the Lord Jesus if you young fellers hadn't come along."

Danny started to speak, but Kit, who had begun to squirm the instant the old prospector mentioned the Lord, cut in quickly. "We'd better be going, hadn't we, Danny?"

Danny looked at his friend and then back at the old prospector. "Do you think you'll be all right, Mr. Harrison?"

"You don't need to worry about me. Now that you got me moved to the kitchen, I'll be fine as silk." He grinned up at them. "I ain't been down for more than three days at a time in my whole life, and I ain't aimin' to start now."

"We'll drop back with your Geiger counter in a few days," Danny told him, "when we look in on you to see how you're making it."

The boys rounded up their mounts and pack mules and started back down the trail toward the place where Mr. Harrison had told them to veer left toward the Wild River.

"At least we know we'll be on the right trail," Danny Orlis said after a time.

"If you can just follow directions," Kit teased.

"Don't you worry about that. Give me some true directions, and I'll show you how to follow them."

"Maybe you'd better wait until we get up to the Bauer land before you start to boast," Kit cautioned. "All you've done so far is talk. You haven't proved yourself yet."

"Maybe you'd better wait until we get back before you boast," Larry put in uneasily. "That uranium is worth a lot of money. That means that Harold is going to be plenty desperate. He's going to do everything he can to keep us from finding out about it."

"You can say that again," Danny answered, shivering. "You should have talked to him on the phone, like I did. There's no doubt about it. He's going to do everything he can to keep us from getting up to that tract of land and finding out what's going on there."

Kit Carson stopped suddenly, his face growing serious.

"I'm awfully sorry, fellows," he said, "but I think I'll be leaving you now. I just remembered that I have a previous engagement."

"Previous engagement!" Larry snorted. "Now, don't give us any of that stuff. Who'd want to have anything to do with you?"

"Oh, I don't know," Kit continued. "I'm not particular. The fact is that it doesn't make any difference who it is, or where. I just want something previous to take me out of here before we happen to run into this Harold guy."

"That's just what I thought," Larry laughed. "Well, you won't get away with it. You're going to stay right here and take your medicine, the way Danny and I are."

"I can tell you both this much," Danny said seriously, "we'll have to watch our step every minute from here on out. If Harold catches up with us here, it'll be just too bad for us."

They forded the shallow but turbulent Wild River and began to pick their way slowly up the mountain slope toward the ridge.

"I'd like to know whether Eric is in on this thing or not," Larry said presently. "I never did hear of the two of them running together, but we both thought we saw Harold in Eric's car."

"From what I hear about Tanner and this Harold, the whole affair sounds as though it's just about his speed," Kit put in sarcastically.

On their way to the main trail, which led to the Bauer land on the ridge, they crossed the swift little stream two or three times as it plunged down the mountainside.

"There's another thing about all this that has me puzzled," Danny said. "If Harold discovered uranium on Ron and Roxie's land, why didn't he just go and tell Dad about it? He would surely be entitled to a good-sized portion of it for having made the discovery."

"I'd never thought of that," Larry answered. "But maybe the law doesn't give any of the find to the fellow who discovers it. Maybe the whole thing goes to the landowner."

"I don't know what the law says," Danny added, "but I know Dad would feel that Harold ought to have a share."

Kit turned in his saddle and looked back at Danny. He shook his head incredulously. "I just can't figure you guys out," he said. "When it comes to money and things like that, you've got the screwiest ideas. Nobody ever gives away any money unless the law forces him to."

"A Christian does what he feels is right," Danny told him, "even if the law gives him an advantage."

It had been shortly after noon when the three boys had left the ghost town and old Jim Harrison. Although they had been pushing their mounts as fast as they could over the rough terrain, they were still less than halfway to their destination at sundown, according to the prospector's directions.

"Don't you think we ought to stop before long?" Larry asked.

"We can't possibly make it up to the ridge tonight, anyway," Danny told him. "We might just as well stop and make camp."

"If that means eat, I'm all for it," Kit said. "I feel like I haven't eaten for a week."

"You might not eat for a week," Danny told him, "if Harold catches up with us."

"You think of the most pleasant things."

Larry and Kit wanted to make camp along the main trail, but Danny insisted that they go up on a rocky ledge, some seventy-five or one hundred feet above the trail.

"Now, what's the idea of coming up here?" Kit asked as they left the trail and began to pick their way slowly up the slope. "There's a perfectly good place to camp right back there by the trail. There isn't any need of coming up here."

"I just don't like the idea of being down on the trail where someone is apt to go past," Danny answered.

"You mean you actually expect someone to come along this lonely trail tonight?" Kit asked him, laughing. "That climb must have affected you worse than I thought."

"I feel a little better up here," Danny said. "We probably won't see anyone, but we do know that this is the only trail down to Scranton and that Harold is going to be traveling it at some time or another. I'll sleep better if we aren't where he's apt to stumble onto us."

"OK," Kit said good-naturedly. "If it will make you any happier, we can camp up here."

They pitched their little tent and took out their sleeping bags. Larry and Kit started to build a fire, but Danny stopped them.

"That's another thing we shouldn't do," Danny told them. "A fire will really give us away if Harold is anywhere in the country."

"But how are we going to cook supper?" Kit protested. "I'm about starved now, and it's a long time until morning.

"We won't have to go hungry," Danny answered. "I think we have enough meat and beans to keep us from starving."

The three of them ate quickly, sitting cross-legged before the opening of their tent. When they had finished, Danny Orlis turned to his cousin.

"I gave my New Testament to Jim Harrison," he said. "Do you happen to have yours along?"

Larry nodded, fishing the well-worn book from his pocket. "I don't know whether or not I'll be able to see well enough to read."

The fading light was so dim that Larry did have trouble reading. However, he turned to the Book of

John and began to read the third chapter. He had heard it so often that he had it almost memorized.

When Larry had finished reading and he and Danny had prayed, Kit said, "I can see why an old fellow like Jim Harrison needs a Savior, but what I can't figure out is why a man like this Nicodemus would need to be saved. Sounds to me like he was good enough. He hadn't been living in real sin."

"The Bible tells us that the biggest sin of all is rejecting Christ," Danny answered. "If that's true, and we know that it is, because the Bible says so, then if we have rejected him, we have committed the worst possible sin, regardless of the rest of our lives. So there aren't any of us who are without sin. We all need a Savior if we want to go to heaven."

There was a long, painful silence. Then Kit got slowly to his feet and walked out among the trees alone. When he came back, half an hour or so later, it was pitch dark.

The day had been a long one, and the boys had had little sleep the night before, so they crawled into their sleeping bags almost as soon as it was dark.

How long Danny had been asleep, he did not know. It may have been three hours, or four, or five. But something, a noise in the distance, like the sound of horses' hoofs against the rocks, awakened him. He sat up in his sleeping bag and looked around in the inky blackness. His heart began to hammer an erratic tattoo against his throat.

The sound came again from somewhere down the trail. Something—or someone—was coming toward them!

TWELVE
Trailing a thief

Danny Orlis lay motionless in his sleeping bag, listening breathlessly. A soft breeze was rustling the pine needles gently, and from somewhere below them an owl hooted lonesomely.

The sound on the trail was so vague and indistinct that it scarcely seemed to be real. He was just imagining things, he told himself. There was no one down there!

And then it came again. He sucked in his breath and listened more closely. It was growing louder.

Stealthily Danny crawled out of his sleeping bag and began to creep barefoot down the trail. The muffled sounds were coming closer and closer, so close that he crouched behind a clump of brush, scarcely daring to breathe. For one minute, then two, then three, he crouched there—waiting.

Suddenly a little circle of light appeared on the trail below him. He bit his lower lip and flattened himself close to the ground. Then he heard voices.

The very sound of them squeezed his heart with icy

fingers and drained the strength from his body. His heart was hammering so loudly that he was sure it must be drowning out the sound of the horses' hoofs. He half expected it to be giving him away. He pressed even closer to the ground as the horses and the little beam of light neared him.

"I don't see why we have to come out here at night, anyway," one of the men said belligerently. "Nobody's going to see us up in this part of the country in the daytime."

"Listen," retorted another voice, which Danny instantly recognized as Harold's, "you've been harping on that ever since we left Scranton. I don't want to hear any more about it. I'm paying you for this job, and you're going to do things the way I want them done and when I want them done. I've tried to make you see that we can't take a chance on this now. If Orlis and those other two guys come up here, they could ruin everything!"

"Orlis!" the other one exclaimed, cursing. "I've got an account to settle with him! I wish he would come up here so I could have a crack at him!"

"Well, I don't," Harold snapped savagely. "I had enough of him this summer to last a long time."

That fellow who was with Harold—it could only be Eric! Danny bit his trembling lip and fought desperately to hold down an almost uncontrollable urge to sneeze. So Eric Tanner and Harold were together, after all! And they were headed for the Bauer land in the middle of the night. Why?

Danny lay there motionless until the two men on the trail had ridden out of hearing and around the bend, out of sight in the thick, impenetrable darkness. Then he jumped quickly to his feet and scrambled back up to where his companions were sleeping.

"Larry! Kit! Wake up!" he cried, shaking them. "Wake up!"

Larry stirred sleepily, rubbing his eyes. "What's the matter?" he asked, his temper rising. "What's wrong with you, anyway? Don't you know it's still the middle of the night?"

"Yeah," Kit muttered, "why don't you go back to bed and let us get some sleep?"

"You won't be sleepy when you hear what I have to tell you."

Quickly Danny reported to them what he had just seen and heard.

"That means there is something valuable up on the ridge," Larry exclaimed, his voice trembling. "Harold has made a strike!"

"Of course he's made a strike," Kit put in. He was wide awake now. "Didn't old Jim say so?"

"What are we going to do?"

"Maybe we ought to go back to Scranton and get the sheriff," Kit suggested. "That Harold is desperate. We haven't any business tangling with him."

"But what would we have to make the sheriff take him in?" Danny asked. "We don't have any real evidence against Harold, the kind that would stand up in court."

"That's right," Larry answered. "Why don't we go on up to the ridge and find out exactly what Harold and Eric are up to? We know they're ahead of us. If we keep our eyes open, we ought to be able to stay out of their way."

"I think you have something there," Danny said. "But they don't know where we are. They won't think of watching behind them."

Kit shook his head. "I'm not so sure about that. Both of those guys are desperate, and they've both been around. They're going to keep their eyes open and not miss a thing."

Larry grinned at him in the darkness. "I'll tell you what, Kit. If you're so worried about going on, why don't you stay here? Danny and I will come back for you when all the fun is over."

"Oh, no, you don't!" Kit retorted quickly. "If you're going up there, I am too. You don't need to think you can get away with leaving me down here all by myself."

Kit thought they should start up the trail immediately, so that they could stay close enough to Eric and Harold to know where they were, but Danny and Larry thought it would be better to wait until morning.

"We've never been over this trail," Danny told him. "And we wouldn't dare to risk having a light, with them so close to us. In the darkness we don't know just what we'll run into. I'd hate to take a chance on a dangerous trail like this one might be."

"No, sir," Larry agreed, "I don't want to start out on a trail in this territory after dark. We'd better wait until it's good and light."

They talked for a few moments, trying to decide what to do. Then they went back to their sleeping bags. Danny tried his best to go to sleep, but every time he closed his eyes, he could see Eric and Harold standing there taunting him or riding along the narrow, twisting mountain trail toward the Bauer land, their horses' hoofs ringing out in the stillness of the night. Finally, however, he was able to drift off to sleep. The next thing he knew, Larry was shaking him.

"Come on, Danny," his cousin said eagerly. "Let's get going. We'll have to hurry over the trail before Harold and Eric finish what they're doing and start back."

Kit Carson whistled at the thought. "Now, wouldn't that be something?" he asked, laughing nervously. "How would you like to go around on one of these narrow mountain trails on the lip of a thousand-foot cliff and come face to face with those two, Danny?"

"I can think of a lot of things I'd rather do," Danny replied, shuddering.

"I can too," Larry added.

The boys scrambled from their sleeping bags and dressed hurriedly in the cool morning air.

"I hate to think of having cold beans again for breakfast," Kit mumbled, more to himself than to his companions.

"I think it would be safe for us to build a fire this morning," Danny said after a time. "Harold and Eric are headed the other way, and the chances are they wouldn't look back long enough to see a wisp of smoke anyway. And besides, if they traveled all night, they're probably holed up in their sleeping bags right now."

Danny took over the making of the fire, showing Larry and Kit how to build a small one in the open with a minimum of smoke. He pulled dry twigs and branches from trees, so that they would not be soaked through with dampness from the ground. In a few moments he had a hot fire going and was frying bacon.

"Doesn't that bacon smell good?" Kit smacked his lips hungrily. "Bacon beats cold beans any day."

"You'd better enjoy it while you can," Danny told him. "When we get up on the ridge, we won't be able to build a fire again."

The boys ate a big breakfast. Before Danny let the fire go out, he fried a double portion of bacon and wrapped it in a piece of paper torn from the loaf of bread. While the water was heating for them to wash the dishes, Larry took his New Testament from his pocket and began to read aloud once more.

Kit Carson sat there quietly, listening to every word. Presently he stopped Larry in his reading of the first chapter of Romans.

"What was that again about the wrath of God and ungodliness?" he asked.

Larry moved his finger back to the eighteenth verse. "For the wrath of God is revealed from heaven against all ungodliness and unrighteousness of men, who hold the truth in unrighteousness," he read.

"What does that mean?" Kit demanded. "I don't exactly believe the way you do, but I think I'm all right. I wouldn't say that I'm ungodly, or unrighteous, either."

"Back in Isaiah we're told that 'all we like sheep have gone astray; we have turned every one to his own way,'" Danny quoted, "'and the Lord hath laid on him the iniquity of us all.'"

He paused for a moment, eyeing his questioner carefully.

"That means," Danny went on, "that we have all

sinned and have turned away from God. None of us are righteous in our own strength. But God laid our iniquity on the Lord Jesus when he died on the cross. So we all need a Savior if we are to have eternal life."

Kit coughed and stirred restlessly. He turned quickly away from his companions to stare out over the green, tree-studded valley which stretched below them. For a moment or two there was an awkward silence.

"Well," he said irritably, "you'd better go on with your praying if you have to do that this morning. We'll have to get over this trail before Eric and Harold finish their business up there and start back."

THIRTEEN
The talking rocks

When Larry and Danny had finished praying, they mounted their horses in silence. Kit did likewise, riding half a dozen paces behind the other two.

Larry and Danny talked about Harold and Eric as they rode, trying to decide how they should go about avoiding them and what to do if they should meet them. Kit was strangely preoccupied. Every now and then when Danny talked to him, he would start suddenly, as though he had not been listening.

Shortly after noon they finally reached the ridge, topped with a huge, towering boulder—the landmark which old Jim Harrison had described to them.

"Well," Larry said almost triumphantly as they finally reined in beside it, "here we are. We made it."

"And we made it without running into our friends," Kit said, laughing. "I'm sort of disappointed."

"Yes, you are," Larry scoffed. "You'd be just as scared as we would be if we met up with Harold and Eric."

"Listen, guys," Danny said, "we'd better find a place

to hide our horses and dismount. If we should come close to Harold and Eric, or if they should come close to us, we don't want our horses to give us away."

"I suppose you're right," Kit said, "but what if we should stumble onto them? If we didn't have our horses, how would we ever get away from them?"

"That's just one chance we'll have to take."

The three boys rode their horses part way down on the other slope, looking for a place where they could safely hide their mounts. They rode for half a mile or so before coming to a natural corral, bounded on three sides by the steep rock walls of a cliff and on the fourth by a swift mountain stream.

They unloaded their pack mules and hobbled them, hiding their food and bed rolls in a safe place, high among the rocks.

More than once they wished for their horses as they climbed back up the steep slope carrying the Geiger counter.

"I don't know whether it was such a good idea to leave those horses down there or not," Kit said. "We'll be so badly out of breath by the time we get up here that we won't be able to run, even if we do stumble on to Eric and Harold."

They walked in a southeasterly direction, staying on top of the ridge and close enough to the trees so that they could dive into them at the first sign of Harold or Eric. They had been walking for an hour or more when Danny first spotted a trail sign.

"Look," he said, pointing to a small, upright, forked branch, which had been driven into the ground to hold up the sharpened end of a twig, about as big as the end of his finger.

"What's that?" his companions echoed.

"I don't see anything," Larry said.

"Look at that sign," Danny told them, pointing again. "Somebody made that as a sign for someone else." He knelt beside the twigs and looked at them carefully without touching them.

"Yes sir," he went on, "somebody wanted to mark a trail."

"Maybe that means something else," Larry said excitedly, reaching for the Geiger counter, which he had been carrying. "Maybe they used this sign to mark a place where they found uranium."

They took the Geiger counter and went carefully over the entire area, but there was no sign of radioactive material.

"Keep that thing out," Danny continued, starting off in the direction in which the twig pointed. "Maybe they used that to mark the trail to the place where they made their discovery."

After going fifty or seventy-five yards up the ridge, they found another Indian sign. Again they brought out the Geiger counter and walked over the area carefully.

"Maybe they were just marking their way to camp," Kit said, after the second search proved unfruitful. "If we keep following these signs, we might drop right down in the midst of their camp site."

"That's something to think about," Danny answered. "We'd better keep a sharp lookout."

The boys moved forward cautiously now, sliding their feet along on the rocks and speaking in whispers or not at all. They came to another forked stick, and another, but the Geiger counter recorded nothing unusual. Finally, about three quarters of a mile from the place where they found the first sign, they came upon two forked sticks, leaning one against the other to form a triangle with the ground.

"Let me see that Geiger counter," Danny said, his voice betraying his excitement. "Maybe this is it!"

Hurriedly he took the small instrument and began to go over the rocky slope. The ticking picked up noticeably.

"Kit!" Danny cried under his breath. "Larry! Come here!"

He moved the Geiger counter closer to the scattered cluster of rock, which was a little smaller than his fist. The telltale clicking began to pick up in tempo.

"We've found it!" Larry cried. "We've found it!"

FOURTEEN
The eavesdroppers

"Do you suppose that's really uranium?" Kit demanded excitedly, squatting beside Danny and Larry.

Danny Orlis moved the Geiger counter away from the rocks and slowly back again. "Listen to the way the ticking increases," he said. "It's working exactly like old Jim said it would when it comes in contact with radioactive material."

"It's got to be uranium!" Larry exclaimed, his voice trembling with excitement.

For two or three minutes the boys looked at one another and listened to the metallic clicking of the Geiger counter.

"It's uranium, all right," Kit said, "but what are we going to do now?

Danny walked slowly along the ridge with the Geiger counter.

"I've got a hunch, guys," he said at last. "It may sound crazy to you, but it just could be right."

"What's that?" Kit echoed.

"There isn't a sign of any digging around here," he went on. "And that doesn't make sense, unless they've found a richer vein somewhere and are working it."

"That sounds reasonable to me," Larry said. "That would be just like Harold, and Eric too. They have this place marked. They probably figure that if they can keep us from finding out what's on the twins' land, they can steal this deposit of uranium too."

Danny straightened slowly. "We've got to find the place where they're working," he said determinedly. "And we've got to do it soon, before it's too late."

The boys were still standing about the Geiger counter, talking, when suddenly they heard the sound of horses' hoofs and voices on the other side of the ridge.

"Somebody's coming!" Danny exclaimed. "Come on! Let's get out of here!"

They ran into the brush and lay there panting. Danny pressed closely against the rocks, his breath coming in short, ragged gasps.

"Who is it?" Larry demanded hoarsely, his mouth almost in his cousin's ear.

Danny turned and shook his head in warning. A moment later two men rode into view.

"Oh, heavenly Father," Danny began, his lips scarcely moving as he prayed inwardly, "help them to keep right on going, so they won't see us here. Keep them from stopping to work this place now. . . ."

"Are you sure you haven't forgotten anything?" Harold Bauer was saying. "A lot of this depends upon you, Eric."

"I know," Eric retorted irritably, "but we've gone

over it a dozen times. I know exactly what I'm supposed to do, and when."

"Fine," Harold said. "But be sure to keep everything straight. And whatever you do, keep those two guys I got to help you from fouling things up. The whole deal's at stake right now. We can't afford to have even a little slip-up."

"Don't you worry about me. I'm not going to make any mistakes. You just be sure that you handle your end of things."

The voices grew softer and softer, and so did the muffled hoofbeats of the horses. Finally they were out of hearing.

"Whew!" Larry exclaimed when they were gone. "That was close! I thought they had us, for sure!"

"I did, too," Kit replied. "If I had been a Christian, like you, I'd have been praying like everything right about then.

Kit had intended his remark for a joke, but Danny answered him seriously.

"I was," he said. "I was praying all the time, asking God to keep them from stopping and to keep us from being discovered."

The tall boy eyed Danny strangely, biting his lower lip.

"What do you suppose they're up to?" Larry put in.

Danny shook his head. "I don't know," he said. "But I know this much—it must be something mighty important, or they wouldn't be going to all the trouble they're going to."

"We found out something else," Kit said. "Instead of two of them, we've got four men to reckon with."

"That means we'll have to be twice as careful," Danny said.

"I was just thinking," his cousin observed. "If we could find their camp and sneak down close enough to it, we might be able to hear them talking and find out what they're doing up here."

For an instant Danny and Kit stared at him.

"It would be easy enough to find their camp," he continued. "We know which direction they went, and we ought to be able to follow their trail."

"That does sound like a good idea," Danny said.

"Oh, but I didn't exactly mean that we ought to do it," Larry protested quickly. "I was just saying that it would be easy to do."

"If we're going to stop Harold and Eric, we'll have to find out what they're doing up here," Danny answered. "I wouldn't be afraid to sneak over to their camp and see what we could find out. They won't be keeping a close watch. They don't know that we're anywhere around."

Larry looked at Danny and then at Kit. "Why don't I learn to keep my big mouth shut?" he asked.

Nevertheless, he was in the lead as the boys slowly and stealthily picked their way through the trees paralleling the path that Eric and Harold had taken.

It was apparent that the two men thought they had successfully frightened Danny and his friends out of town, or at least that they were nowhere in the area, for they rode openly down the trail to the place where they had made camp.

The boys could hear them talking as they sneaked closer and closer. Finally they were close enough so that they could look through the screen of rocks, brush, and trees at the place where Harold and Eric had set up camp. There were two small nylon tents with two sleeping bags in each. The men whom Harold had mentioned were lying lazily in one tent, stretched out on the sleeping bags, with their eyes closed. Eric and Harold were standing beside the latter's horse. "I sure wish that uranium we discovered had been a big strike," Eric was saying. "We'd have all the money we'd ever want."

"My brother's kids would have had it," Harold retorted angrily. "This way will work out even better. We found enough radioactive material to make a Geiger counter or scintillator do handsprings. We can still make a good thing out of it."

"I hope so," Eric said, almost doubtfully.

"Now let's go over this thing once again, Eric," Harold was saying, just loudly enough so that the boys could hear him if they strained their ears. "I'm going to bring those two Denver guys, who started hollering about the uranium stock I sold them, up here day after tomorrow to show them that there is uranium here." He laughed shortly. "Maybe after they see how hard it is to get in here, I can nick them for enough to build a road."

"Do you suppose the radioactive rocks we've scattered will be enough to keep them from going to the authorities?" Eric asked. "You don't think they'll expect to see more of it than what we've got, do you?"

"Listen," Harold retorted, "when I'm through with those two, they're going to think we have the richest uranium strike that has ever been made in Colorado. Just wait until they see that new scintillator go to town on this stuff we've planted. They'll both be begging for a chance to invest some more money with us."

"What about Orlis and his pals?" Eric asked. "What

should I do if they come poking around here?"

"You don't need to worry about them," Harold answered, cursing violently. "I gave him a bad time when I happened to find out that he was flying to Iron Mountain from Minneapolis, while I was there waiting for this new scintillator to be finished. I almost scared him out of coming at all. Then when we found him and his friends that night in Scranton and warned them about leaving town, I'll bet they were so scared that they're running yet!"

"But what will I do if they should come around here?" Eric insisted.

"Turn those guys loose on them," Harold said, jerking his thumb significantly toward the tent where the two brawny men were sleeping. "They'll make Orlis and his pals wish they'd never even heard of these mountains."

Harold swung into the saddle.

"I won't be back tomorrow," he said, turning his horse about. "I'm going to play hard to get. I'll make those two guys think I'm doing everything I can to keep from bringing them up here. Then when I do, I think I'll make them ride the last five or six miles blindfolded, so they won't know for sure where they are."

Eric laughed. "You think of everything, don't you?"

"You have to in this business."

As Harold Bauer rode off along the ridge toward the trail to Scranton, Danny turned to his companions.

"What are we going to do?" he demanded in a hoarse whisper.

FIFTEEN
Hired thieves

The instant that Danny and Larry began to whisper, Kit tugged at Danny's sleeve.

"Don't you think we ought to get out of here before we start talking?" he asked. "Eric Tanner isn't deaf, you know."

The boys turned and crawled slowly back down the slope and to the west, away from the camp. But there would have been no need for them to have been so cautious.

Eric Tanner must have gone directly to his own tent as soon as Harold left. The boys saw and heard nothing of him as they made their way out of the danger zone to a place where they could walk and talk freely without fear of being discovered.

"What do you make of all this?" Larry asked, when they were half a mile or more away from Harold's and Eric's camp.

"I've just been thinking," Danny answered, "about this whole setup. I've changed my mind now. I don't believe that Harold has actually discovered a big uranium find up here."

"What do you mean?" Kit asked him.

"I think he has been selling stock in a phony uranium mine, or on a phony uranium claim," Danny went on. "He has probably collected a lot of money, and now, because he hasn't been carrying out anything, some of the investors are becoming restless. He has made promises to them of quick profits, and now they want to see some of it. So he came up here and planted radioactive rocks in a place where he could find them easily. Now he's going to bring these men, who have been howling for their money, up here to show them that he actually has some land and that he has discovered uranium on it."

"You know," Larry said thoughtfully, "that does fit at that. When he saw that he couldn't get hold of the land for himself, he tried to keep us out of here just long enough so that he could bring these two men up here and satisfy them."

"That could be," Kit agreed, "but if that's all he wanted to do, why did he go to all the trouble of trying to get custody of the twins? Why didn't he come on up here, plant his rocks, bring those men up here, and go on about his business? You, or anyone else, would never have thought about coming out here to look into things if he hadn't made such a fuss about getting custody of the twins."

"You have something there, Kit," Danny said thoughtfully. "Of course, there's an awful lot of prospecting going on out here. He may have discovered a little radioactive material, just enough to make him

110

think that if he had the land, he might be able to make a find on it."

"And," Larry put in, "he might have wanted to have the land in his name so that he could put a real swindle into action. One of the guys was telling me that most of the people who are selling private land up here now are withholding the mineral rights when they sell it, so he wouldn't be able to buy another tract and do the same thing. And he wouldn't be able to sell shares in a bogus uranium mine on government land."

"That sounds more like Harold to me," Danny answered, "and it sounds more like Eric, too. I can't see either one of them being interested in trying to earn money honestly."

The boys walked slowly back to the place where they had left their horses and supplies.

"What do you think we ought to do now?" Larry asked.

"Maybe we could go on down and have the sheriff swear out a warrant for Eric's and Harold's arrest as trespassers," Kit suggested. "That would take care of them and break up this confidence game of theirs until the authorities could get the evidence on them."

"But we couldn't have a warrant made out for trespassing," Danny told him. "We don't own the land. Besides, it isn't posted and never has been. I don't think you could find a sheriff anywhere who would go out and make an arrest under circumstances like that."

"But we've got to do something," Larry put in.

Danny walked thoughtfully over to the little mountain stream and back again.

"If we could just do something to foul up this whole deal," he said, "so that he and Eric wouldn't be able to convince those two investors that they have discovered uranium up here, maybe they would go to the authorities themselves. And they would really have a case."

"Perhaps even Harold will forget where he planted the stuff," Larry laughed. "This country's awfully big. That would certainly foul things up for him."

"Larry!" Danny exclaimed excitedly. "You've solved it!"

Larry Anders looked at him blankly. "Solved what?" he asked.

"You've hit on it! The way to stop Harold and Eric! We're going to move that sign!"

"But," Kit protested, "that's the key to their whole plan. They're sure to know if we molest it."

"These rocks all look alike," Danny told him. "Besides, they wouldn't have marked it if they thought they could find it without any trouble."

"I think it's worth a try," Larry said.

By this time the sun had slipped behind the western horizon, bathing the ridge in shadows. In half an hour or so it would be dark.

"I think we ought to wait until morning, though, guys," Danny said. "We can start out about dawn and take care of it before Eric and his men even crawl out of bed. There'll be less chance of being caught then than at any other time."

They pitched their tent up against the rocky cliff and sat down to eat a cold supper. This time Kit did not complain.

"Boy, I'd rather be hungry than take a chance on

building a fire here and having Eric and his little companions swoop down on us."

"I would too," Larry agreed.

It was too dark by the time the boys finished eating, so they could not see to read the Bible for their evening devotions.

"Why don't we tell about some of the good things that the Lord has done for us, Danny?" Larry asked. "I think it does a guy good sometimes to think about those things."

"So do I," his cousin answered.

Larry began first, telling about how he had accepted Christ as his Savior in jail, just before the sheriff was to take him to the reformatory to begin serving his term. He told how difficult it had been for him down there, trying to live a Christian life among the kind of guys who were there. He told how they made fun of him when they found out that he loved the Lord and was not afraid to testify for him.

"But," he concluded, "I found out then that the Lord is always the closest to us when we need him the most. I found out how he could help me and give me the strength to meet the problems I had. I know that I wouldn't have been able to stand those months there if I hadn't had the Lord Jesus to lean upon."

When it came Danny's turn, he told how he and his friend Jim had gone down into the mountains of Mexico with his Aunt Mabel and how the Lord Jesus had helped them to hide the Bible manuscript which the missionaries were preparing in the native Indian language. He also told how he had helped them to bring it out of the country and up to Lincoln, Nebraska, where it was printed.

Then both Danny and Larry prayed, asking God to watch over them and help them, to touch Harold's and Eric's hearts, and to convict them of their need of a Savior.

When they had finished, Kit Carson looked at them queerly.

"You guys sure have a way of making a guy feel awfully funny," he said nervously, avoiding their eyes. "I feel like I'm about ankle-high to a grasshopper, with all this talk of sin and everything."

"You know, Kit," Larry said to his friend, "that's because God is talking to you about the sin in your life. His Spirit is telling you that you need a Savior."

Kit got abruptly to his feet. "I'm going down to the stream for a drink," he announced, almost belligerently.

With that he strode rapidly away before either of his pals could say another word to him.

It rained hard that night and was still cloudy and threatening the next morning.

"Larry," Kit said cheerfully, "this ought to keep Eric and his little playmates inside while we go out and move that Indian sign."

"I was just wondering if we ought to do it today," Danny said. "After all the rain we had last night, I'm afraid they would be able to see our footprints, if they're observant at all. That might give us away."

The boys waited all that day for the sun to come out. The soil was sandy, and a couple of hours of sunshine would be enough to dry it so that it would leave no trace of their footprints. However, it was cloudy and rainy all that day, and it was not until the following morning that the sun came out again.

"Let's go over there as quickly as we can," Danny said as they finished breakfast. "Harold will be starting back up this way, and if they got a good early start this morning, they might be here shortly after noon."

They washed their dishes and started through the woods to the place where Harold and Eric had planted the uranium and the forked-stick sign to mark it.

"What if he decided to come back yesterday?" Larry asked as they neared the site. "What if Harold is over here already?"

"We'll just go up and say, 'Pardon me, Mr. Bauer,'" Kit said, "'haven't we met somewhere before?'"

Danny and Larry laughed a little, nervously.

It seemed to the boys that it had taken them several hours, the other time they walked along the ridge, to reach the place where the radioactive rocks had been scattered. But this time it seemed as though they were there almost before they realized that they were well on their way.

"Well, there it is," Danny said, pointing up the ridge to the first Indian-type sign. "Now to get to that radioactive material and move the sign before anyone shows up."

Danny hurried on ahead. In four or five minutes he had reached the place where the two forked sticks had been thrust into the ground. Hurriedly he picked them up and strode along the ridge and down a few paces to another spot, about two hundred yards away. By the time Larry and Kit reached him, he had the sign set up exactly as it had been before.

"Now," Danny said softly, "we'll see how well Harold can find his uranium."

At that instant a harsh voice from high on the ledge above them rasped, "All right, Orlis! Don't move!"

Danny and his companions whirled to see Eric Tanner and his two burly, ill-tempered helpers standing there eyeing them.

SIXTEEN
Captured!

For a moment Danny Orlis stood as though he were frozen. He stared up at Eric Tanner, his face ashen. Cold beads of sweat stood out on his forehead.

"All right, Orlis!" Eric shouted angrily. "What are you doing here? Start talking!"

"Come on, Danny!" Larry cried, diving into the brush.

Danny and Kit tried to follow suit, but the instant that Larry moved, the two men came hurtling down the steep, rocky slope. One of them grabbed Danny and Kit by the arms, and the other hurried past them toward Larry. He grasped Larry by the collar and jerked him to a stop.

"Where you think you going, huh?" he demanded in broken English. "You not go so fast when Joe get you."

"Take it easy," Larry managed. "You're choking me!"

"You're lucky I not choke you with my hands," the one called Joe blustered. "Now get over there, and stay, or you're gonna get hurt! And don't you give me no trouble, either." He shoved Larry ahead of him back to the place where Danny and Kit and their captors were standing.

Larry struggled to free himself, and Joe gave him a shove that knocked him sprawling.

Larry scrambled to his feet, eyes wide with fright and his whole being as taut as a steel spring.

"Shall I, boss?" Joe asked, looking toward Eric hopefully. "Shall I, boss?"

"I ought to turn Joe loose on you, Larry," Eric said, cursing savagely. "And if you give me any back talk or trouble, I will! I don't have to take anything from any of you!"

"Should I hit him one boss?" Joe asked again. "Just to show him what he get if he don't be good?"

Eric Tanner ignored the big thug who stood towering over Danny's wiry little cousin.

"Now, I'm going to ask you some questions," Eric said gruffly, "and I expect some mighty straight answers. What are you doing up here? How come you're snooping around up here on the ridge?"

"The land belongs to my brother and sister," Danny explained, striving to keep his voice under control. "We came up to look around."

"Well, you picked a mighty poor time to do any looking around," Eric snapped. "I can tell you that much! How come you picked this particular spot to do your snooping?"

Kit Carson looked at him. "Is there any better place around here to snoop, Eric?" he asked.

Tanner cursed angrily.

"Come on, Joe," he ordered. "Let's take 'em back to camp! And if they give you any trouble, let 'em have it!"

118

Danny Orlis took a quick, hurried glance about, as though hoping against hope for a chance to escape from his captors.

Kit looked over at him and shook his head. "Not a chance, Danny," he whispered softly.

The instant he spoke, Eric Tanner whirled around to stare at him, his eyes flashing darkly. "You guys, keep your mouths shut!" he ordered. "I'll tell you when you can talk!"

He took Danny and his companions east along the ridge to the place where they crossed the slope and headed down to the camp which Harold and Eric had set up.

"Now, if you do what you're told, you won't get hurt!" he snapped. "But if you don't, I don't want to be responsible for you. You'll get just what you ask for." He turned to Joe. "All right, Joe. Tie 'em up!"

"You don't need to do that to us," Larry protested.

"Oh, don't we? We'll see about that."

Joe jerked the ropes savagely about their wrists until the stiff fibers cut into their flesh.

"You're not gonna get loose, I betcha," Joe boasted to Danny. "You tied up now. You tied tight."

"You've got my wrists tied so tight that I think you've stopped the circulation," Danny protested.

"If you don't shut up, we'll tighten them again," Eric told him.

Eric Tanner had been calm, even boastful, as he directed the two burly henchmen whom Harold had left to help him. He had laughed when Larry cried out in pain as Joe tightened the rope about his wrists.

"Why don't you call on that Lord of yours to help you get your wrists untied, Anders?" Eric asked, laughing coarsely. "You talked Peggy into tossing me overboard because of him. Now let's see him help you get loose."

Larry looked at his captor evenly. "I'm putting my trust in Jesus, Eric," he said. "I know that he's watching over us."

Eric snorted and said something under his breath. Then he turned and stepped out of the tent.

He had been calm enough before, but now that the boys were securely tied and in the tent, he paced nervously from one end of the camp to the other. Every now and then he stopped to look down the trail with a pair of field glasses.

"He must be expecting Harold back any minute," Danny whispered softly after a time.

Kit nodded.

"He's as nervous as a cat."

Larry had bowed his head and was praying earnestly in silence. Danny did the same.

"Do you really believe that your Lord will help you get out of a mess like this?" Kit asked presently.

"Of course he will," Danny answered. "The Bible tells us that he hears and answers our prayers and that he will do anything we ask that is in accord with his will. I've had a lot of prayers answered, Kit."

Eric, who heard them talking, looked in.

The boys stopped talking until he went on again.

"What would happen to you if—if Eric really did turn those guys loose on us?" Kit asked.

"I'd go to heaven," Danny said simply, "and so would Larry."

Concern flashed across his face. "But what about me?" he asked.

Danny was silent for a moment. "The Bible tells us," he began, "that there is a place prepared for those who haven't taken Christ as their Savior, for those who haven't confessed their sins and made themselves right with the Lord. That place was also prepared for Satan and his angels."

Kit swallowed hard. All his bravado was gone.

"But does God really care about us?" he asked. "Does he actually care what happens to you and me?"

"Of course he does," Danny told him. "God cares so much for us that way back there, nineteen hundred years ago, he sent the Lord Jesus, his only Son, into the world to live a sinless life here, die on the cross, and be raised again, so that you and I and everyone who will confess his sin and put his trust in Christ can be saved. That's how much God thinks of us."

There was a long silence.

"I—I—" Kit stammered, his face showing something of the turmoil that was churning in his heart. "I've got to do something about Jesus," he said, his voice taut. "I can't go on like this."

"It's so simple," Danny told him. "Do you feel that you are a sinner and need a Savior?"

Kit Carson nodded. "I always thought I was a pretty good guy before," he said softly. "But since you guys have been reading out of the Bible and talking about what it means to be a Christian, I've come to see that there's so awfully much in my life that isn't what it should be. I want to make it right, Danny. But I never could live good enough to be a Christian. I just know that I couldn't."

"God doesn't expect us to," Danny answered. "He knows that in our own strength we can't live the way a Christian ought to live. But we don't have to do it in our own strength. If we put our trust in him and have faith that he has the power to save us, he counts that as righteousness, or being good."

"And as far as Christian living is concerned," Larry said, "if we trust in the Lord Jesus and ask him to help us live in a way that is pleasing to him, we'll get help for that too."

Eric Tanner strode to the tent just then and thrust his head inside.

"All right, you guys," he snapped irritably. "Pipe down in there."

They sat silently in the little nylon tent until Eric moved away from the door. Then Kit looked first at Danny and then at Larry.

"Guys," he said softly, "I want to be a Christian."

The three of them bowed their heads together and prayed. Kit's prayer was short and halting, the prayer of one who was unfamiliar with the Lord. When he finished, Larry and Danny prayed, asking God's blessing upon him.

Kit smiled crookedly when they had finished.

"You know," he said to them, "I haven't said anything to either of you about it, but I've been so upset about this thing that I haven't been able to sleep or even think about much of anything else. You don't know how good it is to have the matter settled."

"Oh, yes, I do," Larry replied. "It wasn't so awfully long ago that I went through the same thing myself."

Danny moved a little, as much as the ropes tied about his legs would permit him to move, and looked out the doorway of the tent. Eric Tanner was standing on a rock, sweeping the trail intently with a pair of high-powered field glasses.

"You see 'em yet?" Joe demanded gruffly. "You see the boss?"

"There's somebody coming up this way," the boys heard Eric reply. "I can't quite—yes, I believe it is. That's Harold's horse, and there are two others with him."

Eric turned and started hurriedly back toward the tent. Danny Orlis closed his eyes quickly. Larry and Kit did the same.

"All right, you guys. I'm going to gag you, and I want to check those ropes again. I'm going to see that nothing happens to let you fellows foul this thing up!"

SEVENTEEN
A narrow escape

Quickly Eric Tanner tied strips of an old dish towel about the boys' mouths, gagging them securely. Then he looked at the ropes on each pair of wrists, giving them a savage tug.

"I did a good job," Joe said, sticking his head in the tent. "They not come loose."

Eric nodded grimly.

"Yes, you did a good job, Joe. These guys won't get loose to spoil things now. You and Pete stay here and watch them. I'll go and meet Harold." He turned back to Danny and his companions. "If you boys try any funny stuff, it'll be too bad for you. Understand?"

All three of them nodded vigorously.

"I gave Joe instructions to watch you," Eric went on. "He's not too smart, but he knows that when I tell him I want something done, he'd better do it."

For a few minutes after Eric had gone, Danny and Larry and Kit sat motionless in the tent. If ever they were to get away, Danny told himself, it would have

to be now. The minute Harold left with the two investors, Eric would be back to help.

With a quick look out the tent door to be sure that
Joe and Pete were not watching them, Danny scooted
around until his back was toward Kit. He moved his
hands, which were tied behind his back, significantly
up toward the gag on Kit's mouth. In a moment or
two the new Christian understood what Danny was
thinking of trying.

Quickly he moved his head forward and down until
the knot that held the gag in place was at Danny's fin-
gertips.

Feverishly Danny worked, feeling the hard knot
with his sensitive fingers and working as best he
could to loosen it.

"Oh, Lord Jesus," he prayed as he worked, "help me
to get this gag off. Help me to loosen it!"

Three minutes, then four, and then five passed.
Danny's arms throbbed, and his tired fingers were
trembling. But finally he managed to untie the knot.

"There!" Kit exclaimed thankfully as the gag fell off.
"I didn't think you'd be able to do it. Now I'll see if I
can untie your hands."

Kit took the rope in his teeth and began to work
slowly on it, feeling the twists in the rope with his
tongue. Joe had knotted it tightly, and it seemed to
Kit and Danny and Larry that it would never come
undone, but finally he managed to get the knot half
out.

His jaws ached, and for a moment or two he sat
there, biting hard and working his jaws. Then he
went at it again. At last Danny's hands were free.

He tore the cloth from his mouth and hurriedly undid the gag that bound Larry.

"Now let me get those hands untied," he said excitedly. "We don't have any time to lose."

He went to work with his jackknife, cutting through the knots to loosen both Larry and Kit.

"Now what are we going to do?" Kit asked.

Danny edged silently to the front of the tent and peered out through the flap. Joe and Pete were lying on the ground with their eyes closed.

"I don't know whether they're sleeping or not," Danny whispered, "but we don't have time to wait to find out."

"What are we going to do?" Larry asked, his voice quivering.

For answer Danny took his pocket knife and sliced a long opening in the back of the nylon tent.

"Come on, guys," he said. "We don't have any time to lose."

Hurriedly they slipped out of the slit in the tent and scampered silently up among the rocks. Hastily they scrambled over the ridge and down among the trees on the other side, putting approximately one hundred yards between them and the two men who were supposed to be guarding them.

"Won't those guys be surprised when they wake up and find out that we're gone?" Kit asked, laughing silently.

"I'll laugh at that one when we get safely back to Scranton," Larry muttered under his breath.

"What are we going to do now, Danny?" Kit asked again.

"We'd better go back to where our horses are

hobbled and get out of here just as fast as we can," Danny told him. "We don't want to be around when Harold and Eric find out that we're gone."

The boys picked their way hurriedly among the trees until they thought they had gone beyond the spot where Harold and Eric had sprinkled the radioactive rocks.

However, as they approached the top of the ridge, they realized that Eric and Harold and the two investors were just on the other side.

"There must be something wrong with this scintillator," Harold Bauer was saying. "We had an excellent reading here a week or so ago."

"I don't think I ever heard of anything going wrong with one of those," one of the investors said irritably.

"If you brought us way out here, Mr. Bauer, and now pull something like this on us," the other one cut in, his voice rising in anger, "it's going to be too bad for you. We're going to look into this. We'll get to the bottom of it. And don't you forget it."

Harold looked helplessly at Eric.

"Does this look like the place to you, Eric?" he asked.

The younger fellow glanced quickly about.

"I don't think it does, Harold," he said. "I believe we were higher than we are now—higher up on the ridge."

With that he took the scintillator and began to stride dangerously close to the place where Danny and his friends were hiding. The three boys melted among the trees, and not a moment too soon, for Eric strode past the spot where they had been and stopped with the scintillator close to the ground.

"Here it is!" he cried.

The three men ran over to where Eric was standing and stared at the scintillator.

"Look at that!" one of the investors cried. "Just look at that! We're rich!"

Danny, Larry, and Kit melted farther back into the forest and began to hurry toward the place where their horses were tethered.

Not a minute later Pete and Joe came running toward the men.

"Boss!" Joe shouted. "They're gone! The kids are gone!"

For the space of a heartbeat the boys stood rooted to the spot. Then Larry started to run as fast as he could. Danny and Kit followed him, scrambling over the rough ground.

They fell, sprawling on the rocks, only to leap to their feet and run again.

"Are you sure?" Eric shouted, the sound of his angry, frightened voice ringing through the trees.

"Sure I'm sure," Joe retorted coarsely. "One minute here and the next gone."

"What kids?" one of the investors demanded. "What kids are you talking about?"

"The kids that—" Joe was stopped by a withering glance from Eric.

"There were some kids who were hired to come up here and snoop around," Harold Bauer said. "The party who hired them thought a kid or two wouldn't be so apt to attract suspicion. They got wind that we were on to a big strike, and they wanted to try to get it away from us. If we don't catch them before they go down to Scranton and file a claim, we might lose our strike."

"Nobody would use kids for that kind of business," one of the men said suspiciously.

"You don't know what people will do when uranium is involved."

"But I thought you owned this land," the other one said. "If you own the land, what's this business about filing a claim?"

For an instant Harold's face blanched. "Do you know anything about the laws governing a uranium find?" he demanded angrily. "Well, I've made a study of it, and I tell you, if those kids get down to Scranton before we do, we'll lose this strike!"

"Well, come on, then," one of the men exclaimed, starting toward his saddle horse.

"You fellows go back and saddle up your horses and begin to look around the ridge," Harold said to Joe. "We can't let those kids go down to Scranton."

"Why can't we go now?" one investor demanded. "We'd better try to beat them to the courthouse if what you say is true!"

"What I say is true, all right," Harold almost shouted, "but I'm running this thing. And we'll do things my way! Eric, you go with Mr. Harding, and I'll go with Mr. Gerard. If you see those kids, don't let them get away!"

The boys were running as hard as they could run now, scrambling over rocks and fallen branches as they plunged down the slope toward the stream.

"Our only chance is to get to our horses before those guys catch us!" Danny panted.

The high altitude was telling on them. Their breath was coming in long, tearing gasps, and their hearts were hammering fierce tattoos against their chests. But they did not stop! They could not! Every moment in that race toward their horses counted desperately.

Finally they reached the little patch of grassland where they had left their mounts and pack mules with their supplies. Quickly they caught them up, threw on their saddles, and started to ride.

"We'll have to go a long way around to keep from crossing the granite spine of this ridge," Danny said under his breath as his horse started to ford the creek.

"Harold knows that if our horses are on this side, we'll have to go across, so the chances are that he has stationed someone on the ridge to watch for us."

With a desperate prayer for guidance and wisdom in their hearts, the boys rode through the dense forest. The going became rougher and rougher, and the trees were thicker and closer together the farther they rode, but still the granite ridge that they had to cross lay above them.

Finally Danny turned to his companions.

"We've got to risk it," he said tensely. "We've got to take a chance and cross the ridge."

Danny rode on for thirty or forty feet, then turned his horse toward the gnarled, rock-strewn ridge.

"Are you guys ready?" he whispered.

They looked at one another and nodded.

Danny leaned forward and urged his horse up over the bare rock. His companions followed.

EIGHTEEN
Riderless horses

Danny Orlis and his companions kicked their horses savagely in the flanks with their heels and plunged headlong down the ridge toward the main trail.

"I saw them!" Eric shouted from somewhere behind them. "Come on, guys! We'll head them off!"

Danny leaned low over his mount's neck urging her faster and faster. From somewhere behind he could hear Eric and Harold and the others crashing through the trees as they sought to come between the boys and the main trail.

"We won't make it!" shouted Kit. "They'll get there first!"

For a moment or two the boys rode on, clinging desperately to the backs of their hard-running horses.

"You heard what old Jim Harrison said about these horses going home if they were turned loose, didn't you?" Danny called back to Kit and Larry. He kept his horse at a driving gallop.

"Sure thing," Kit managed, "but what does that have to do with us now?"

"Let's send our horses on ahead," Danny suggested. "Eric and Harold and the rest of the gang will follow them. That'll give us a chance to get away."

"But if we let our horses go, we'll never get out of here," Larry protested.

"It's our only chance," Danny told him.

Their pursuers were some three or four hundred yards behind them among the trees.

"OK," Danny said under his breath. Scarcely slowing their horses, the boys swung off, rolling on the ground as they landed. Fortunately no one was hurt, and they scrambled to their feet and tore down the tree-covered slope to put as much distance between them and their pursuers as possible. The frightened horses were running at top speed, and Eric and Harold swept by in a desperate effort to catch them before they reached the trail.

"Man, that was close!" Larry panted as they ran. "Another half minute and they'd have had us."

"What I'm wondering," Kit said without slackening his pace, "is what we're going to do when they catch up with those horses and find out that we're not on them!"

"I'm hoping those horses will keep right on going," Danny answered. "And with all that shouting and yelling behind them, there's a good chance that they will, at least for a while."

Larry slowed to a brisk walk.

"We can't keep that up the rest of the way to Scranton," he panted. "I don't care if Harold and Eric are after us."

For two full minutes the boys did not speak. At last their breathing slowed, and the color began to come back into their cheeks.

"Maybe we can slip over to Jim Harrison's," Danny Orlis suggested. "He could tell us the quickest—" He broke off suddenly.

A hundred yards or so in front of them a man on horseback appeared and headed directly toward them through the trees. They looked around frantically, but there was no place to go, no way to escape.

"Well," he said, smiling, "so you're the boys we're looking for!"

Danny swallowed hard and nodded. His tongue was thick and dry, and his hands were trembling.

"Were you looking for us?" Kit asked innocently.

The investor, whom they had heard Harold call Mr. Gerard, smiled at him.

"We've been doing a lot of wild riding over this mountain looking for someone," he said. "But I certainly didn't expect to find you fellows here. I thought you were on horseback."

"I think our friends, Harold and Eric, are in for a little surprise after a while," Gerard went on, chuckling as though someone had just told him a good joke.

"You don't have to rub it in, Mister," Kit replied defiantly.

The man looked down at him, a kind expression on his face. "I don't mean to be rubbing it in, son," he said. "In fact, I mean just that. You see, we've had several complaints about Harold Bauer's operations—selling uranium mine stock. We asked him some routine questions and didn't like all the answers he gave, so we decided to make a more thorough investigation."

Danny eyed him quizzically. "Just what do you mean by that, Mr. Gerard?" he asked respectfully. "Who are you, anyway?"

"I guess I didn't tell you boys who I am," he said, taking his wallet from his inside pocket. "I'm from the state sheriff's office. We have reason to believe that Harold and his friends have been obtaining money under false pretenses."

"Whew!" Danny gasped. "I guess Harold and Eric are in for a surprise!"

The deputy state sheriff said, "I think we've got you fellows to thank for breaking this thing open for us."

"What do you mean?" Larry asked.

"Well," he went on, "this land was in the name of a Bauer, and he claimed to be representing the estate. He had been very careful in what he told those whom he sold stock to. He told them that there was risk involved and that he didn't want them to buy any if they couldn't afford to lose their money, in case things went wrong. You would never have guessed that he was selling worthless stock, and I guess most of the people whom he talked to believed that he was on the level."

The deputy dismounted and stood beside the boys.

"But why did you come up here?"

"Well, we bought some stock from him a few months ago, after hearing his sales talk, and began to press him for some returns, to see what he would do. When he brought us up here and showed us his findings, I was beginning to believe that the guy was on the level. He took a lot of pains to tell us that he didn't know what was going to happen, or what we would find—that all the way through it was a risk. Everything went fine until you boys escaped. Then he became panicky and went to pieces."

"We were the ones who kept him from finding

uranium at first," Kit said, "when he had you guys up there. He and Eric had put out some radioactive material and had marked it with a little sign. We found it with our Geiger counter and moved their sign."

Mr. Gerard laughed heartily. "That was another thing that made me suspicious," he said. "When Harold couldn't get a reaction on his scintillator, he went to pieces. It looks as though you boys had more to do with that than I thought."

"But," Larry put in, "what should we do now?"

"Let's go back up to the main trail," he said. "Eric and Harold and those two thugs who are helping them have probably caught up with your riderless horses by this time and are coming back to look for you."

"Where's Mr. Hardin?" Danny asked.

"It was his job to stay with Harold," the sheriff replied. "He'll be along with them."

It was a week later. Harold and Eric and their two helpers were safe in the jail in Denver, and Danny and his companions were sitting in the kitchen of the ghost town hotel, talking with Jim Harrison.

"Yes, sir," the old prospector said, picking up his cane and tapping it lightly on the floor, "I sure never knowed what was going to happen when I saw you boys riding into town."

"You weren't the only one," Kit laughed. "We didn't know what was going to happen either, when you stuck that rifle of yours in our backs."

Old Jim started to laugh, cackling in a thin, high-pitched voice.

"I'm going to let you in on a little secret," he said,

lowering his voice. "I never had any idea of hurting you. And I never really figured you had anything to do with them fellers that was fixin' to put in that road."

"Then what were you so worked up about, Jim?" Larry asked.

He laughed again. "You know something, Buster?" he went on. "A feller gets awful lonesome up here living by himself this way. I just figured on having a little fun. Thought maybe I could make you go back home and tell everybody about the crazy old coot up in the ghost town."

They all laughed at that.

"I'm mighty glad you helped catch them fellers," Jim said, changing the subject. "It's guys like them that make it hard for an honest prospector to get himself a stake."

"We won't need to worry about them for a long while," Danny said, sobering. "With all the charges that are filed against them, they'll be lucky to get off with twenty-five years in the pen."

"I've been wanting to ask you something, Danny," Kit broke in, "but I just never happened to think of it when you were around. Did you get to talk to Eric—about his soul, I mean? You said that you were going to before they took him to Denver."

Danny nodded. "I talked to him for a long time," he said, "but it didn't do any good."

"What did he say?" Larry asked.

"He said that we were about five years too late with it," Danny answered. "He thinks he's too far gone for God to possibly save him."

"Did you tell him about me, Buster?" Jim Harrison

asked. "Did you tell him about the old feller up in the mountains who had lived for Satan all his life until just a few days ago? Did you tell him that I confessed my sins and let Jesus take them away?"

"I tried to, Mr. Harrison," Danny told him, "but he wouldn't listen."

The old prospector shook his head sorrowfully. "We'll have to be praying for him, fellers."

The three boys nodded in agreement.

"The only thing I regret," Jim went on, talking more to himself than to his visitors, "is that I didn't become a Christian fifty years ago. Maybe I could have done something for the Lord."

After trying out his trout streams for a day or two, the three boys helped the old prospector fill his wood-bin and water pails and then said good-bye.

"You know," Danny said as they rode away, "I sort of hate to go back to the Angle and tell Dad that there isn't going to be either a road or uranium for the twins." He took a deep breath. "When I look back, the trip seems almost useless."

"Don't say that," Kit put in quickly. "Look at old Jim Harrison and me. If you hadn't come out here, the chances are that neither one of us would have accepted Christ as our Savior."

"It just goes to prove," Larry said softly, "that all things work together for good to those who love God."

THE DANNY ORLIS ADVENTURE SERIES

DON'T MISS ALL SIX EXCITING BOOKS ABOUT DANNY ORLIS AND HIS ADVENTURES!

The Final Touchdown
The Last Minute Miracle
The Race Against Time
The Showdown
The Case of the Talking Rocks
The Sacred Ruins

If the Danny Orlis series is not available at your local bookstore, you may call Tyndale's toll-free number **1-800-323-9400, X-214** for ordering information. Or you may write for pricing to **Tyndale Family Products, P.O. Box 448, Wheaton, IL 60189-0448.**

Tyndale House Publishers, Inc.
Wheaton, Illinois